ZANDER
&
ELLA

W. WINTERS &
AMELIA WILDE
WALL STREET JOURNAL & USA TODAY BESTSELLING AUTHORS

PLAYLIST

Little Do You Know – Alex & Sierra

Me and My Broken Heart - Rixton

Mercy - Brett Young

Renegades - X Ambassadors

Ho Hey - The Lumineers

Little Talks - Of Monsters and Men

All Your Exes - Julia Michaels

Without Me - Halsey

Overwhelmed - Royal & the Serpent

Love is never wasted, for its value does not rest upon reciprocity.

– C. S. Lewis

From USA Today best-selling authors W Winters and Amelia Wilde comes a sinful romance with a touch of dark and angst that will keep you gripping the edge of your seat … and begging for more.

I was born into luxury and used to getting what I wanted.
What I desired most, with my life in disarray, was the man who sat across from me.
He was tall, dark and handsome, but, most notably, forbidden.
It made every accidental touch more sinful
and every session more addictive.

There was so much tragedy and he was supposed to fix me.
I shouldn't have wondered how it would feel to be trapped under his broad shoulders.
I shouldn't have focused on the way he licked his bottom lip every time his gaze dropped from mine and roamed my curves.
I shouldn't have dreamed about him breaking the rules to comfort me the way I desperately needed.

I did though, and I was the first one to break.
He was my protector and my confidant and then he became my lover.
I teased him, tempted the two of us and now there's no way to take it back.
With everything I've been through, I didn't expect to fall for him.
There's only so much heartache I can take.

Hold Me

PROLOGUE

ZANDER

Distracted and rattled, the world outside blurs by until it resembles a seemingly fake movie set. With the driver side window down and the wheels spinning against the asphalt highway, I'm barely conscious of anything at all. Other than her. My Ella.

None of this seems real. I can't help but to think that this can't be happening. My heated palms twist against the leather steering wheel as my fingertips go numb and that sinking feeling settles in my gut. It's as if I could punch the fronts of the buildings and they'd fall down, one by one, until the whole town was leveled. It all must be fake. It can't be real.

With last night's darkness behind me, a pale pink hue settles along the horizon.

The sun's coming up, but it's a cruel joke now that they've made the decision to separate the two of us. I've spent the last three weeks of my life anxiously waiting for the sun to set so I could go back to her. Now I'm caught in a morning I don't want, driving on autopilot back to a motel I know won't aid in giving me rest. Barely seeing the road.

It's not the first time I've felt like this. It's like being forced into the past. It feels as though I'm being forced into another horrific incident that would keep me up at night.

Blinking away the memories, I slow as I come to a yellow light, my gaze flicking to the rearview and I spot Damon, still behind me. Swallowing thickly, I remind myself that I can never go back. It's not possible and even if I could, I might not be able to change a damn thing.

There are things we can control and things we can't. The horrible losses we suffer—at times—come from our own actions.

Last night, I slept with Ella. Thoughts of last night flash before my eyes, images of her beauty stealing my breath, and remembering her soft moan of my name heats my chilled blood. It was against the rules. It was against everything we stand for at The Firm.

I lost control.

Something about her makes me *want* to lose control. It makes me *need* to lose control. I want to lose myself in her and come out the other side a different man. Smirking sardonically, I breathe out heavily and move past the green light as my blinker ticks, ticks, ticks away the thought. It's all another cruel joke from the asshole that is the universe. I'm different now, and I hate this person. I'm running to get away from this morning and the memories of that other morning. Both of them push forward in my mind, tangling up with one another.

A sickness pulls the corners of my lips down as I remember the past I wish I could forget. A past that made me this weakened version of myself.

Bang! *There's a loud knock at my apartment door that calls for my attention.* Bang, bang, bang. *Another three in a row.*

"You want me to open it?" Damon's eyes hid the worry he felt as equally as the exhaustion. We'd been up all night at my place. Waiting for her after searching everywhere and calling everyone.

"Mr. Thompson, it's the police." The deep voice echoes in my mind in a way I know I'll always remember.

The leather sofa groans as Damon makes a move to stand. "I'll get it," he tells me as I stare blankly at the front door, a sick feeling running rampant through me. The cops don't show up at anyone's apartment this early in the morning unless something fucking terrible has happened.

It hadn't been twenty-four hours, so I couldn't make a missing persons report. The second I heard that knock and the officer's voice, I knew there would be no report. I knew there would be no search. I knew that much, and still, I didn't want it to be real.

My throat's dry as I turn down the street I've taken for the last three weeks with nothing but anticipation to see Ella. My distraction, my drug, my submissive and … more. Something that's hard to place. Something I don't dare look into, for fear of the depths of its meaning.

I didn't hear a damn thing they said that day two years ago. I was too focused on how numb I felt and how it couldn't be real. How much my heart hurt, even though the rest of me was detached and unfeeling. When the guilt hit, it hit like a sledgehammer. Afterward Damon had to repeat everything they'd said. He was the one who told me about the mugging. About her murder. About what happened to Quincy.

I'll never forget our conversation after she told me to give her space on that street corner.

"I want to be with you." Quincy's blue eyes shone with tears, but she didn't let them fall. She stood her ground on the concrete and looked up at me with her arms folded over her chest. "I want more."

My response was short and immediate. "That's not where I am." The words seemed inadequate, and they were.

"But someday—"

"It's not going to happen." I thought she'd appreciate honesty. After all, it wasn't her fault. I didn't want more and I didn't know if I ever would. But her eyes fluttered shut for a brief second, the pain setting in, and when she opened her eyes they were cold.

"I'm going for a walk." The iron chair grated against the sidewalk, the streetlights outside the bar providing nearly all the illumination in the late night. I'll never forget how they cast shadows down her face. She would be in tears within minutes. I knew it and I hated myself for it.

"I'll walk you. You don't have to say anything to me."

She held up a hand. "I need space, Zander. If you don't want to be close to me, then I need space. Don't follow me. If you don't want all of me, then I don't want any of you."

I didn't follow her. I had another beer, the cool summer breeze and the guilt keeping me there, wondering if she'd turn around. She didn't. After forty minutes, I left, figuring she'd gone home and hoping I'd find her there. The thing I dreaded as I walked was the thought of her packing up her things. Even knowing I couldn't give her everything she wanted, I didn't want to lose her.

I waited for her to show. We'd fight about it, I thought. We'd argue, and she'd make her case, and I'd make mine. I didn't love her like she did me. I didn't want a fairy-tale wedding and children. I wanted what we had and I would be happy to stay there, like we were, for as long as she wanted.

Three hours into the darkest part of the night, I started calling her and then two more hours slipped by. The digital clock of the cable box barely moved as time crept by and I was met with voicemail after voicemail. Every place was closed by 3:00 a.m. There was no reason for her to be out that late. She never answered. Then I called her friends, her mother. I called anywhere and everywhere I could think. Damon and I went out to look for her and came up with nothing. We came up with nothing because by the time we were looking for her, Quincy was already dead.

A car honks loudly behind me. Through blurry vision I move my gaze from the rearview that features a line of cars behind me, to the green light above me. Easing on the gas, I bring myself back to the present.

Back to Ella. To them trying to take her away from me. And keeping me from her.

Unacceptable.

The fact they took her doesn't change the way I feel for her or what either of us wants. It doesn't change a damn thing, except my standing with The Firm. And perhaps The Firm will take a hit to its reputation … but that pales in comparison to what Ella and I stand to lose.

Part of the reason I let Quincy walk away from me that night was because I was too much of a coward to have the real conversation. The one that would end with her moving out, deleting my number from her phone and never speaking to me again. I was trying to honor her wishes for space, but in truth I was acting like a fucking coward because that conversation had been long overdue.

I can't honor anything for Ella, because I don't know what

she wants now that they all know.

I don't know if she's imagining I've abandoned her, or that I slept with her and never looked back. I don't know a damn thing and that's also un-fucking-acceptable.

What kind of man would I be if I went back to the motel and left it at that? If I let men who aren't part of our relationship decide it was over because of my professional obligations? What kind of coward would I be?

I jerk the wheel to the right at the next intersection, my mind racing. My blood pumps hard in my veins. This isn't that night with Quincy. This is a different morning. A far more complicated relationship. I didn't know what I wanted with Quincy. I *have* to be with Ella. That is the only thing I know right now.

That's the truth. The one truth that keeps me sane.

In the rearview mirror, I watch Damon's car come after mine, his tires squealing. He's swearing in the front seat, his expression pissed, and that anger won't leave once he finds out what I intend to do. What I have to do.

If Ella doesn't have feelings for me or if she doesn't see any need for me at all, then I'll leave her be. I'll let her go on with her life. I'll step back and allow her the space to get well. I'll never bother her again.

But I'm not going to take anyone else's word for it or allow them to make that decision for her. My heart slams against my rib cage over and over and over. Her manager and the rest of The Firm can claim she doesn't want to see me all they want. I'll believe it when she tells me and not a moment before.

They'll have taken her to one of the properties The Firm hires out in conjunction with every client. We always have a backup safe location in case the need arises. It's typically nondescript. Meant to keep from drawing attention. We still followed this protocol even though Ella is a custodial client and not someone needing strictly personal protection services.

It's a few miles from here. Not far although I've driven a good distance in the opposite direction.

Another sharp right and I'm heading in the right direction. Damon honks behind me. He'll know where I'm going. He doesn't have any choice in the matter unless he decides to crash his car into mine. That's the only way I'll stop.

CHAPTER 1

ELLA

This sinking feeling in my chest is one I haven't felt for a long time. A very long time. I'm not unfamiliar with the sickening churn in my gut or the heaviness that presses down on my shoulders, begging me to cave to it and make myself small.

After the last year and a half, I'm quite used to its abuse and the screaming that accompanies it in the back of my mind. This particular feeling, though, is one that used to come often as a child. I imagine so many people feel it. All of us, really. The gut instinct that warns a child they're in trouble. That they've done something very wrong and disappointed the ones they love.

The memory of my father's dark eyes narrowing as I stood

there, my fingertips fiddling with the hem of my shirt or my sleeve, forces me to swallow although my throat is dry.

The men surrounding me aren't my father, but they have authority over me and it's not until now that I feel both immense regret in this decision and an anxiousness as I question the consequences of my impulsive actions. It's all too much.

The expression on each of the men who sit across from me tells me disappointment is only one of several emotions. Anger, betrayal ... Concern. Kamden's fidgeting, and his readjusting in the simple black mesh office chair next to me makes me even more uncomfortable.

He's barely looked at me. None of the men have since I sat down. It's eerily quiet and the squeak of the wheels rolling as Silas takes a seat next to Cade marks the first noise I've heard apart from someone clearing their throat.

I woke up expecting to find Zander, but his shift had ended and instead Silas waited for me downstairs. He was polite but firm that I should dress quickly. Silas was my driver to this less than appealing meeting.

He's been vague and his tone far less pleasant than it typically is.

My heart may be rampaging, beating against the cage that contains it, but I endeavor to keep my shoulders squared and my expression emotionless, neither positive nor negative. Even if every man in this room wears a stone-cold expression to match the dark gray of their power suits.

I could have worn black for mourning and to reflect this deep-seated emotion that brews inside of me, but that's uninspiring so I opted for a dark red silk blouse and high-waisted skinny jeans. Red is a color of confidence.

"What's this about?" I question and my gaze is drawn to Cade's throat, the cords of it tightening before my eyes travel back up and he offers me a tight smile.

"It's about your relationship with Zander." Kamden's voice is low, cautious even. There's a ping that runs through me. It's sharp, like swallowing a thorn, and keeps me from answering immediately. That churning in my gut intensifies as I meet Kamden's gaze and then Cade's. It's a horrid feeling that, in this particular moment, can fuck right off.

"What of it?" I reply in a harsher tone than I'd have liked. I've never desired to be a "bitch" so to speak, although I hate that word. I might not be a fighter and I might hate confrontation, but that doesn't mean for one second that I can't defend myself. A side of me that I haven't felt for years returns.

In the silence, I question again, "What of it?" Cade recovers quickly, but I don't miss the shock in his dilated pupils.

The man himself looks worn thin. Bags under his eyes match those of Kamden's, if I'm honest. Silas focuses on his clasped hands in front of him, not reacting at all to anything. If I could read minds, I'd wager a bet he'd rather be anywhere other than here.

With a heat simmering along my shoulders, I wait for any of them to speak. Kamden repositions in his seat yet again and then places his hand over mine. I don't react to the contact; instead I stare at a dull painting of black and gray smears that's hung on the wall behind Cade as Kamden speaks. It's a modern piece that would fade into any room. Surely it's only meant to take up space.

Clearing his throat, it's obvious that Kamden is the one who will initiate this conversation. "Mr. Thompson crossed a line," Kamden starts and that brief sentence grants him my full attention.

My expression hardens and I can't help it. I'm quick to rip my hand away from under his. My bottom lip trembles as betrayal overrides every other emotion. I desperately wish I could control myself more in this moment and not allow the shock and despair to show at all because I know emotion doesn't work with men. In this room, I'm the one who lacks any power at all. My guardians and conservator have all the power they want over me, yet I can't help but scoff, "*He* crossed a line?" In that instant, under Kamden's unwavering expression of concern, I consider, for a moment, that Zander's done with me.

That I was foolish to feel more and think there was more between us. We slept together, he told them, and now he's done with me.

It wouldn't be the first time I thought a man wanted

more than just a fling. The thought is an ice bath but I'm quickly relieved of that submersion when Kamden says, "I placed cameras in the living room ... I know he took advantage of you."

I feel sicker as his admission sinks in. This is a new kind of hell. A bloody nightmare. One I can't escape.

"You put cameras ...?" I can't finish the question; there's no more air in my lungs. *He put cameras in my home? Kamden spied on me? My Kamden? The one man I can remember who I've trusted all my life?* The questions race through my mind. It's not possible. "You wouldn't do that to me."

Cade says something, confidently even, not that I hear a damn word. Kamden's blue gaze doesn't leave mine. We're caught here, staring at one another as we come to terms with our new reality. I hope Kam can feel this, this burgeoning sense of betrayal brewing through me. It's hot and suffocating. My eyes prick and I hate it. I hate that he's done this to me.

I expect a lover to break my heart, but not Kamden.

"Yes. I put cameras in the house to—" His voice is even before I cut him off, although his expression is anything but. There's a sorrow there that I've seen before. Only once, but it's the kind of sorrow that comes with the fear of losing me.

"And you say Zander crossed a line?" It takes everything I have to push out the accusation as I stare at my dearest and closest companion. My bottom lip wobbles again and I have to bite down on it, closing my eyes out of frustration. My hands tremble and I pull them into my lap.

"You know I did it because I love you," he practically whispers and I'd forgotten about the other two onlookers until one of their chairs protests as they readjust in their seat. I'm not sure which one it was, and I couldn't care less. Let them watch. Let them know what it's like to betray me.

"You spied on me." My voice comes out in a low hiss as I raise my eyes to Kamden. I'm seething with anger.

"You … I can't trust … I …" Kamden stumbles over his own words and I struggle not to break his gaze. He does it instead. He's the first to look away and seems to second-guess himself.

"That fucking hurts," I say, biting out the words.

My moral high ground is swiftly taken away from me as Kamden's exasperation reveals itself. "What do you want from me? The last time I left you alone—"

Raising my voice I can no longer control, I tell him, "I wasn't alone!" Heat rolls down my spine. "This time," I add to clarify and lower my voice. "I wasn't alone."

"No. You weren't." Kamden doesn't back down, and his lowly spoken words are harsh.

"It's not like I didn't want him."

"He's supposed to take care of you," Kam says.

"Since when does sex not fall under that umbrella?" My response is flippant and arrogant, and Kamden reacts with equal parts disbelief and outrage.

"Since you tried to kill yourself!"

My throat instantly dries and my attempt to swallow is painful as I lean farther away from Kamden. My lips part to object, but there are no words.

"You aren't ... You aren't okay," Kam says, his voice gentler now, and his hand raised as if he's approaching a wild animal. "It was wrong of him to touch you in any way. He was only there to make sure you didn't hurt yourself. That was his *only* job. He crossed the line multiple times and I can't ignore that. You matter to me. Your safety matters to me."

His only job. A sarcastic huff leaves me although my fight has waned. The first time I saw Zander, I wanted him. I was drawn to him. A piece of me needed him. It didn't have a damn thing to do with a job opportunity.

In my silence, Kamden repeats, "He was supposed to take care of you, protect you. Not sleep with you."

Was. Kamden speaks of Zander as if he's in the past tense.

They're going to take him away from me. I can hardly breathe. I would beg them, if that's what they want. I will beg them. It takes a moment for me to gather my composure and my dignity.

Licking my bottom lip, I muster the courage to look Kamden in the eye and tell him, "I'll tell the judge it was all of you."

My words are met with a deafening silence. "I'll tell him each one of you abused me."

"Ella." Kamden ushers his warning in a whisper.

"Not you ... but if you make me, I'll tell the judge you knew." If I'm not above begging, I'm damn sure not above blackmail, defamation, or whatever the fuck this is. "You won't take him away from me."

CHAPTER 2

ZANDER

The city was going by in the background without making any impression before, but now it's in vivid detail. My main priority is getting to Ella. There's an anxiousness I haven't felt for her before. A need to protect her.

I know the situation is complicated, but this part seems simple. Get to her. Get to her. Get to her. I ignore my phone vibrating in the passenger seat; one glance in the rearview and I know it's Damon calling.

Friendship be damned, I won't make the mistake of not fighting for her to have a say in this. If nothing else, she deserves to hear from me and know this wasn't my choice.

With the tires screeching and my nerves still rattled, I pull into the parking lot six minutes later. The office is on the top floor of a two-story building. We chose the location because we considered possible press coverage when we designed her protection plan. She's not unknown to the world, and no matter how slim the chances, we had to prepare for everything. It's harder to take photos of a person when they're not at ground level.

It's then that I consider what exactly I'm about to walk into. I can already feel the betrayed gaze of my brother and the sick feeling that comes with it.

The second the car door shuts with a *thunk*, my name is shouted from Damon's car pulling in beside me. In the shade of the towering building, a chill settles over me and I ignore Damon, I ignore the gut instinct to give my brother space now that he knows what I've done.

Instead, one foot moves in front of the other, but not fast enough.

Damon throws himself out of the driver's seat so fast that the door hangs open after him. "You can't do this," he shouts although there's a pleading tone in his voice. We're both angling for the entrance, and he collides with me as I'm reaching for the door. His shoulder is pressed to my shoulder and I'm met with a desperation in his gaze as I can feel his chest rising and falling with heavy breaths. The momentum takes me a few feet away but I'm determined. "Zander. You can't go in there. You're off her detail." His voice is low and careful, but again, his tone is begging me not to go in there.

For her sake or mine? Maybe both. "Your brother said you can't—"

"That doesn't fucking matter. I'm seeing her, and you can't stop me." With my hand wrapped around the steel handle of the black glass door, Damon's splays against it, preventing me from opening it. The sleeve of his coat slides down his forearm.

"You're caught, man. Nobody's going to let you do anything until Cade figures shit out. We might have to have a hearing if Kamden pushes this, which—to be fucking blunt—I would if I were him. And even if we don't and everything blows over, The Firm can't let you see her." His dark eyes are wide. He presses his free hand flat to my chest, pushing me back and I release my grip on the handle, dropping my arm to my side. He's at least as strong as I am, but he knows better than to square up with me.

More importantly, I want this more than he does. I want to get in more than he wants to keep me out. "We can't let you see her."

Gritting my teeth and reining in as much anger as I can, I push out, "That's not up to you. She has control over her life. You can't forbid me from seeing her."

"We can. As a member of The Firm—"

"Then I'll fucking quit, if that's what it takes. None of you can unilaterally determine that I'm a threat to her if she *wants* to see me. And I'm not going to stop." My breaths are deep and slow, although my pulse is raging in my ears.

Even if adrenaline is coursing through my veins, my mind is clear. I'm only focused on this. Getting to her. To hear what she has to say.

"You know just as well as I do, that doing this could hurt her," I say, reminding him of his duty as her therapist. "Ripping away someone who was helping her."

"Zander ..." My name comes out like a warning as he shakes his head.

Damon can pretend it's not in her best interest, but it is. It's a crucial component to her healing. If they keep us apart when she doesn't want that, it could send her spiraling. "If she needs me in there, you're fucked. You know that, right? If taking her away from me compromises her health, you are fucked. Try explaining that to the judge."

"Zander—" I reach around him and he catches my wrist in one hand.

I break his hold. Of course I do. I've trained for this, same as he has, and something in the movement must tell him that I'm serious because he backs off half a step, his hands up. "Did they change the location of the safe house?"

His lips form a thin line. I'm being a dick right now, and I know that. He's not supposed to tell me anything about Ella's location. Private citizen or not. Member of The Firm or not. But we've got a lot of history between us.

"You can refuse to tell me if you want, but I'll just search every building in the city until I find her. I'll search the whole damn world."

Damon lets out a breath, defeated. "They didn't change it. She's upstairs as far as I know."

My next step forward is determined, emotions I didn't expect spurring me on.

"Just—" Damon moves to block me. "It's not good, Z. They've got proof of what you did. This isn't going to turn out well for you, and it might destroy the rest of us. It would be better if you went back to the motel and let Cade handle it. If you did that, maybe there would be a way to figure things out. I don't know."

Swallowing thickly, I nod, acknowledging that I know I put them in jeopardy. "If it goes to court, I'll testify none of you knew a damn thing. That I doctored the security footage so no one else would know about us."

"Just stop—"

"You don't get it. I'm not leaving her up there." My throat goes tight, my heart beating too hard to be contained. "Things aren't finished between us. This is about more than what I want. Hell, what I want doesn't mean a damn thing right now. She tells me to back off, and I will. But I have to know. I have to hear it from her. She gets to make that choice."

"Let's talk about it for a few minutes first," Damon says and irritation rolls through me. He takes a few steps in the direction of the cars, away from the door. "Make sure you're calm. It won't do anyone any good if you go in there with that look on your face."

"What fucking look?"

"Like you'd pull down this building with your bare hands to get to her."

I pause. Hope brightens Damon's eyes; he thinks he might have convinced me to stay out here and have a pointless conversation with him.

"Listen," he says. "You did this, but we can figure out what to do—"

I don't hear the rest. I've yanked the door open and I'm sprinting inside. Punching in a code on the keypad in the foyer. The door clicks open. They haven't changed it yet. Thank fuck.

"Wait," he shouts behind me.

I don't.

I'm halfway professional by the time I get up the stairs, Damon breathing hard behind me. I've at least arranged my face into something I think resembles professionalism. But as I shove open the door, I know how skin deep it is. Underneath I'm feral.

They're arranged around the table of the conference room and there's a deadly atmosphere in the room. The tension is palpable. A reception desk takes up one side of the space. A sofa and two chairs huddle around a bean-shaped table in the corner. Silas on the left. Kamden on the right with Ella beside him. Cade looming over everything at the head. I almost missed Dane, standing outside the conference room. He didn't make an effort to stop me and judging how he's opted out of this meeting, there's something happening with him that I'm not aware of. I don't have time to give a fuck about that.

They're all in suits. And I'm still dressed in my overnight shift clothes. Faded black jeans and a matching T-shirt.

All of it drops away when I meet Ella's dark eyes. They flare wide and my heart aches. She didn't expect me to come for her. Is it surprise in her eyes? Relief? Or maybe horror?

In a scrambled effort she backs away from the table, the wheels of the chair rolling back as she attempts to stand. "Zander," she says, and my name has never sounded so good as it does right now. "Z." Kamden puts his hand on her arm like that asshole is going to keep her in her seat, but she shakes him off. Her legs work to carry her around the table as fast as she can go and she flies into my arms.

The office erupts. Damon curses behind me. "I tried to stop him," he tells the others, and I don't care.

The feel of her body in my arms makes everything and everyone else fade into the background like white noise. It pushes away a number of things I don't expect to feel. I breathe in the delicate scent of her skin, and run my hands over her shoulder blades. Over her back. Her heart flutters in her chest but her arms are tight around my waist.

I want to keep her in the circle of my embrace, where nobody can touch her but me. To protect her and give her the choice of what's next. Cade's warning command to leave falls on deaf ears. He repeats my name and clears his throat. From my periphery I'm faintly aware that he's standing now. There's movement behind me but I ignore it all.

There's something I have to do first.

I put my hands on her shoulders and create the only space I can bear between us. Tipping her face to mine so I can look into those dark eyes, she's trembling but she looks as determined as I feel. Ella's stronger than people give her credit for. Maybe even stronger than I gave her credit for.

"I tried to come back to talk to you this morning. Last night—it wasn't a mistake for me." I have to choose my words quickly, and carefully. I could get cut off at any time. "I want to be with you. I need to know if you want the same."

She pauses, and it's the longest moment of my life. It drags out and out and out until my entire life feels like it's hanging between us. Her eyes stay on mine, searching there, and Ella swallows. It reminds me of the first time I saw her in that courtroom. How quiet she was. But she knew what she wanted then too. And I think she knows now. She gives a single, subtle nod.

Before my brother can make it to us, his footsteps foreboding, I tell Ella to sit, leading her back to the table and pulling her chair out for her. It's silent in the room as she gracefully does as I command. She can't hide the gentle simper at her lips and it forces a heat to run through my chest.

Pulling out the chair opposite to where my brother was seated, I join the meeting like I belong here.

"I fucked up," I announce to the room, but I'm looking at my brother, who's retaking his seat, his narrowed glare not leaving mine. "I crossed a professional boundary. My emotions became involved and I should have told someone before things got this far. I should have come to you."

"You didn't," Cade replies and then swallows so loud I can hear it from across the room. He's shaken and looks like hell. There's an edge to his voice so sharp it lowers the temperature in the room. "You didn't do that, Zander. You had an inappropriate relationship with a client. You can't be part of this anymore."

"I apologize." He breaks the hold he had on me, his gaze dropping to his hands as he clenches his jaw.

"But it would be a mistake to discontinue our relationship, as its purpose has been meaningful to her mental health. I'm certain any one of you can attest to the fact that she has ..." It's uncomfortable speaking about Ella while she's sitting next to me, able to hear every word.

"I've been," she says, pausing to take a deep breath, then lifts her head to meet Damon's gaze. "Healing."

Everyone turns their heads to look at Ella, whose cheeks go pink. There's color in her face. A brightness to her eyes that wasn't there when she stood at the front of the courtroom. She's visibly healthier. She's been revealing more about what drove her to the unfortunate place she was. "I'm doing the work that needs to be done," she adds firmly.

"I'm not asking to be in charge of her care. I'm asking to stay in contact. It's my opinion that cutting off contact between the two of us would have a negative effect on Ella's health. That's my top priority."

Cade arches an eyebrow at me. "Is it?"

"Yes." I've felt how Ella has come alive in my hands, and I'll be damned if I let her go back to that desperate shell of a woman. "Her well-being is my top priority. Same as it ever was. And I know I failed you, Cade. I should have informed you of how our relationship had changed, and I didn't. I knew it was wrong to go behind your back. But it's not wrong for us to continue this relationship."

"What are you asking me to do?" Cade's expression is hard, and admitting that I have royally screwed him over hasn't softened it. But there's something in his tone that speaks to the fact that we're brothers. He won't let my break from protocol be the final determination.

"I'm asking you to give this a chance. To have the conversation about what it looks like for me to stay in contact with Ella. That's what I'm asking for."

ELLA

"And as I've just indicated before we were interrupted, I'm not above extortion."

"What?" Zander's expression hardens as he stares at the side of my face. I keep my gaze fixed directly ahead on Cade's expression. I wonder if I hadn't just threatened each of the men in the room, how they would have responded to Zander's request.

Swallowing down the anxiousness of Zander discovering what I've just done, I keep my hands steady on the table and remind the room what I'm capable of.

"If I'm no longer able to speak to whomever I want, to see whomever I want, and ..." I say, barely peeking at Zander from the corner of my eye. The five o'clock shadow along his hardened jaw sends a wave of want through me. I've never wanted to kiss him more. "... I'll tell the judge each of you slept with me." I dare to raise my gaze to Cade's, whose own widens yet again before he narrows his eyes at me. "I'll tell the judge you used me, each of you, however you wanted."

"Ella," Kamden scolds in a hiss.

"Well, I'm out of my mind, aren't I?" I bite back at him. "I can't possibly know what's right and wrong, isn't that so,

Kam? So if I'm unable to choose who I want to fuck, and how ... I can't be responsible for my accusations, can I?"

The condescension drips from my words. "There's evidence of course that I've been sexually active. And apparently a video as well." The last part is reserved just for Kamden.

In the silence, I take a moment to relieve the tension that runs chaotically through me and then meet Cade's gaze.

"You will do no such thing." The drop in Zander's voice and the dominant tone in his cadence send a thrilling heat along my skin.

My expression doesn't betray me. I remain as poised as I can and turn to meet Zander's gaze. It blazes with the threat of a punishment.

We speak at the same time. Him: "Do you hear me?" Me: "Understood."

With my heart rampaging and my lungs refusing to let me breathe, I straighten my back and wait for whatever is next.

Butterflies stir in my stomach when Zander's hand lands at the back of my neck, and his strong grip there is comforting more than anything. Then he runs his thumb along my skin and as he speaks, his words are lowered and meant just for me as he leans closer to me, although I'm certain every man in this room can hear. Zander tells me, "That is—not only— unnecessary, but an act that obviously requires a thorough evaluation when we meet next."

Thump, thump. With the pounding in my chest and a

heat pulling at my core, I nod and whisper, "Understood."

It's only when Cade and Kamden both begin speaking that I cut them off to question the room, "And when will that be?"

Glancing to my right, I meet Kamden's disapproving gaze and downturned lips. He doesn't speak and it spreads an uneasiness through me.

"Why don't we all take a moment?" Cade questions, his attention split between his brother and me.

"A moment?"

"Ella," Kamden whispers, competing for my attention, but I remain submissive to Zander.

"I'd like to speak to my brother."

"I'd like to know when—" I begin to say but Zander speaks calmly, interrupting me with an assuredness I desperately needed to hear from him.

"Go, Ella. I will fix this. Go home."

There's a numbness that takes over as he relaxes into his chair, facing his brother as I've been effectively dismissed. He offers me a covert, kind smile as if it's reassuring, but I don't want to leave.

"I feel like I should stay," I whisper and I don't recognize my own voice. It begs for permission.

Zander's hand flexes, the motion drawing my gaze as his fingers spread wide before forming a fist. It's his warning signal for me to behave. Heat flows down my shoulders instantly.

Sucking in a breath, I attempt to collect myself as I stand

slowly. It's then that Zander reaches out, his hand meeting my thigh with a tender touch.

"I will be there tomorrow. I promise," he tells me and with that I can finally breathe.

As I prepare to leave, glancing at Silas and assuming my driver here will be the one to take me home, Kamden stands behind me.

"I'll drive you," Kam comments and I turn to face him and his sharp blue suit. It's custom tailored for him and meant to appear expensive, which it does. But Kam looks nothing but beat down.

My gaze drifts between a nodding Zander and Kamden.

My throat tightens as I leave the room, attempting to lead the way, but Kamden opens the door for me.

The clicking of my heels beneath me is all I can hear as I follow Kam in silence. As I climb into the passenger seat of his car, not even the sun can offer me warmth.

I hadn't even considered sitting in the back, as I never have before with Kam—not in all my life—until the seat belt clicks and his keys jingle as he slips them into the ignition.

I can barely stand to look at him without feeling like I've been stabbed in the back. Taking in a shuddered breath, my hair flattens as it meets the headrest and I attempt to relax into it. The gray stone wall shrinks in the distance as he backs out and we leave The Firm behind.

"Nothing to say?" I barely breathe, the words attempting

to stay buried inside of me but somehow I pull them out.

All I'm met with is the ticking of the turn signal and a heavy exhale. Another minute goes by and Kamden hesitantly asks, "If he hurt you, you would tell me, wouldn't you?"

Turning my head to give him my utmost attention, I swallow down every emotion and answer him simply, "Yes."

He nods shortly and continues to drive, although the atmosphere in the car is suffocatingly broken.

CHAPTER 3

ELLA

The morning after what seems like war feels nothing like victory. Even if you've won. It's as if I'm terrified to drop my guard, ready for the next hit. Taking into account everything that's happened over the last three years up until just yesterday, it's all felt like fate's been toying with me, but also like dominoes toppling. One after the other, each one poised to fall, starting on that day I watched James step onto the crosswalk.

And now I wait on edge for the next piece of the game to forsake me.

Pushing my hair still damp from the shower away from my face, I try to tell myself it can get better. It doesn't have to be like this. A constant spiral downward.

Although sleep didn't come easy, the anxious ball in the pit of my stomach has left. Even after I took the sleeping pills Aiden had prescribed, it still took another hour or so before I had a dreamless rest.

Damon's towering figure steals my attention from the steam of the teacup. It billows out as I blow gently across it, both of my hands wrapped around the porcelain vessel.

"Did you sleep well?"

Giving his suit a once-over, I make a mental note that he's back to business attire. Ever so serious. Damon was the one I was certain would speak up for me. Instead he said himself, he tried to stop Zander.

The cup clinks softly when I set it down on the counter as I answer, "Once I got to sleep, it was a deep sleep." I can't look at him, but at least I've given him the truth.

My father told me once, when I was much younger, that if I didn't want to fight, if I didn't want to feel the blows of incoming war, that I had to stop. I couldn't keep my hands up, prepared for battle, and expect the other side not to react. It's one of the hardest things I ever had to learn: to stop fighting. Although Damon told me it's called decompressing.

Apparently I don't decompress well.

Damon pulls out the stool beside me and the legs of it groan against the floor.

Gently, I push a tray of danishes his way.

"Kamden?" Damon questions and I nod.

"I'm not sure where he is, I've only just come down," I explain to Damon, "but they were waiting for us."

I've already eaten two of the small cream cheese danishes. Damon opts for a raspberry one, taking a piece off with his left hand, holding the rest of it in his right. Before popping the small morsel into his mouth, he asks, "Did you talk to him?"

I turn on the stool to face him and lean my elbow against the counter. Half of me feels nothing but comradery with Damon, and the other half doesn't trust him anymore. I'd like to speak, but instead I shake my head and focus back on my tea.

It's the perfect temperature and has steeped just right.

"Is it all right if I ask if you're angry with him?"

"Yes," I answer quickly, the word raw. Then I realize that only answers whether or not it's all right if he asks me. "I'm very upset."

"Angry and upset?"

It takes me a minute, staring down at my tea before I answer, "Just upset."

Damon nods and I glance over to find he hasn't eaten any more of the small pastry.

I offer him an out. "This can wait, you know? Quiet mornings are one of my favorite things in life."

Instead of nodding and backing off, Damon asks, nearly blurting it out, "Are you upset with me?" His deep brown eyes sink into mine and I'm forced to stare back at him.

I nod and then whisper, "Yes. Honestly, I am."

"I am sorry yesterday caused you distress. I'm sorry it all happened the way it did." His words seem sincere but also professional. As if reading my mind he adds, "I mean it, Ella. When they told me what happened, I was worried about how it would all play out, but mostly worried about you."

Finally breaking his gaze I murmur, "I appreciate that," and return to a now empty tea cup.

It's a bit awkward for a moment, until I pull an open package toward me and inform Damon, "This was waiting for me too."

I take out a chunk of gray crystal. The dark and light grays mingle with a touch of white.

"What's that?" Damon questions.

"It's a rock." Removing the note from Kelly, I read it to him. "Smoky quartz wards off negative thoughts."

As Damon rises, making his way around the counter to the sink, I tell him Kelly sent it and that she suggested I bring it to therapy.

The charming grin on his handsome face grows and that small, amiable feeling takes over. Damon has an infectious smile. "You told me about Kelly? Didn't you?"

As I nod he tells me, drying off his hands, "I like her."

Smiling, I agree with him. "I've got good friends." The admission comes with a sinking feeling that steals the lightness from me. Damon doesn't miss it. Before he can say a word, I tell him, "I think I need a minute."

With a more somber look, although his eyes remain warm, he says, "When you're ready to talk, let me know."

An hour after breakfast the sun sits perfectly in an array of pale coral hues along the tree line. Pulling a blue chenille throw across my lap, I do nothing to stop the breeze from blowing across my bare shoulders.

My satin sleep shirt boasts the same cobalt blue.

It's quiet in the late morning, although I know it won't be for long.

"You brought tissues?" Damon questions, taking the seat across from me on the patio. The outdoor fireplace is to his right but it's not nearly chilly enough to turn it on. Maybe later tonight.

"They're still here from last night," I comment. The square box of tissues and journal sit side by side. Both were used equally last night. Silas gave me space, he's good for that. Quietly watching, checking on whether I could use tea or anything to offer comfort. He's kind and silent. Damon is kind as well … but never silent.

"I think last night might be a good place to start."

"Last night it is then," I respond and let out a sigh, repositioning myself on the chaise lounge to better face him. I'm caught off guard by his next question.

"Do you think there's any chance that you're displacing your feelings?"

"What do you mean?" I ask.

"Your husband with Zander."

"How is that relevant to last night?"

"It's relevant to all of it, Ella."

"So that's what we're doing today?" I say with mock humor. "We're sparring?"

"We're discussing my one concern." Damon remains professional, giving me a moment to consider my answer.

I don't want to think about it. I don't want to go anywhere near that question. Am I displacing my feelings toward James, my deceased husband, onto Zander? That's a heavy question to begin a session with. "It feels like fencing," I mutter, feeling more uncomfortable by the second.

"Is that what you'd like to talk about?" Damon raises his brow. "Fencing, or maybe we can talk about croquet?"

"Croquet?"

Damon shrugs and says, "It seems like an equally relevant sport."

His comment is rewarded with a short and relatively quiet bubble of laughter I can't control, and I readjust in my seat.

"I know we've talked about this before, but it's okay to sit with your emotions. Right?"

I nod in response, pulling my knees into my chest and making myself a puddle of blue fabric, none of which can protect me.

"Why do you want to come between us?" I question him.

"I don't," he answers without hesitation and he's adamant. With both his hands on his knees, he leans forward in the seat across from me, shaking his head slightly while maintaining eye contact. "He's my friend and ..." he pauses, glancing away and trapping his bottom lip between his teeth before seemingly deciding what to say next.

With a deep breath in, he continues, "I have no issues with you engaging in sexual activity." I've never felt such a guard rise between the two of us. Him considering my relationships and whether they're a concern for him creates an unnatural tension that Damon doesn't seem to notice. The only person who should be concerned about who I'm fucking is me. With my fingers tangling together in my lap, I gather my composure. I know his concern is only for my mental health. I know it, yet I struggle with him being involved at all with that part of my life. Zander is mine. It is irrelevant what anyone thinks of us and our relationship. He wants me and I want him. That is all that matters.

Damon's voice, no longer droning, comes back into focus when he says, "I noticed an immediate change for the better when you two began your relationship. I spoke to Zander at length last night. He's updated me on any essential information."

My heart skitters knowing Damon spoke to him, but I

haven't. My cell phone sits on the coffee table and I hesitate before picking it up only to find that I still have no messages. To date, the only person to text me or call me on this ancient brick with no camera or apps has been Kam.

"Please know I only asked what was required professionally."

"Hmm?"

"When I spoke to Zander," he clarifies and I absently nod, not liking the knots that sit in my stomach. "There is no judgment from me."

"It certainly feels like there's judgment," I comment, staring back at his umber gaze.

There's a moment, a tick of time between us before Damon tells me, "My only concern was how quickly things changed."

If only he knew how I slowly unraveled since the moment I first saw Zander. How I felt myself come undone for him before he ever touched me. I question confiding in him, so instead I remain silent.

"How do you feel right now?" he asks.

"Angry." My response is immediate and my throat tightens with it.

"Angry … What size, would you say? A little irritated anger?"

"Enraged," I answer, staring down at my hands.

"You don't seem enraged," Damon responds carefully, like he's testing me.

A well of emotions dries out my throat even further. "Sad ... scared."

Damon nods as I answer. "And why's that? What triggered those emotions?"

I put myself in this position. I'm in this place because of what I've done. Tears leak from my eyes and as I wipe them away, refusing to be overwhelmed by them, the back door opens.

Kam pauses when my eyes meet his. His black T-shirt and worn black jeans initiate a smart-ass side of me, as well as a piece still bitter from Kam's betrayal. "Feeling down today?"

I don't miss Damon's ever-watchful gaze as I pull myself together and then stare up at Kam, who glances between Damon and myself.

"Are you?" Kam turns my question back at me. "Am I interrupting?" Kam asks Damon and I'm quick to answer, "No."

I can't look either of them in the eye.

"Just one minute if you don't mind," Damon says, then looks between the two of us and Kam nods, slipping his hands into his pockets as he walks to the edge of the paved patio. With a deep inhale I let go of everything, every wave that threatened to drown me just a moment ago.

"A little homework?" Damon's voice is gentle and low, far too soft for Kam to hear.

"Homework?" I offer him a smirk but then nod, closing my eyes and preparing for whatever it is that Damon wants.

"When you feel overwhelmed or uncomfortable or like you're losing control, like what happened just now," he says without judgment, yet my eyes whip up to his, "I want you to ask yourself, what emotion is it? Take control of those emotions that make you uncomfortable. Because you long for that, don't you? Control over those emotions?"

I can only nod. I don't want them to control me. In this moment I know he understands. Damon understands. The moment he leans back in his seat, it's like a spell has broken and Kam's footsteps can be heard nearing us.

"Are you all right?" Kam's question comes from a place of concern and I shrug.

"A wreck like always," I tell him.

"You're never a wreck." Kam consoles me, taking the chair next to Damon and when Damon begins to stand, Kam asks him to stay.

"I came out to speak to you, really. With Ella's consent."

My brow knits and matches Damon's confusion for a moment. "I want to make it clear that whatever it is Ella wants, whether The Firm stays, whether Zander continues to see her ..." Kam's gaze moves to me as he continues, "It's her choice and I will back her up."

Damon's posture remains relaxed although his brow cocks and his head tilts. "Whatever she says?" he asks without amusement. I imagine the threat of extortion is riding through him and I feel bad for the man.

"Kam, I don't think that's necessary."

"I was wrong and I'm going to make it up to you."

Damon's uncomfortableness is more than noticeable in his deep exhale.

Kam continues, "Whatever Ella decides to say, I saw and heard it as well."

"You realize that's not only a crime, it also could be detrimental to her healing."

Kamden doesn't flinch until Damon's concern about my health is spoken.

The defensive tone comes with Kam shifting in his seat. "This is her life. Her decision."

Damon's careful with his response, his posture casual although I'm more than aware he's a master of controlling his body language and speech. "We both want what's best for Ella, and I imagine we won't have any issues moving forward."

"That all depends on—"

"Am I a bit fucked up?" I say, interrupting the men. "Yes." It takes a lot for me to utter the next words. "Watching your husband die only feet from you could do that to someone." Tears leak and I wipe them away. "Seeing the video of it repeatedly every time I turned to social media, having to talk about it constantly, having to beg people to stop ... it got to be a little much, I'll admit." The words come out a whisper. Even now, as I sit here, I see it all over again.

The red light, his smile as he waved, leaving me to the

paparazzi. He had the most charming smile. The stifling heat of that summer day weighs down on me and it comes with an anxiousness I can't stop. The sound of the truck, the tires locking up, I hear it all, the screams from onlookers and then my scream. I feel the hands that held me back, those fingers digging into my skin now.

My voice is hoarse as I look each of them in the eye and say, "Am I a threat? To anyone? To myself? I don't know but I don't want to be, and I'm trying."

Both of them part their lips to say something, to coddle me, to praise me ... To admonish me, maybe. I have no idea, nor do I give a fuck.

"Is Zander bad for me? No. He's not. So stop threatening to take him away. We're adults. We know what we're doing. Stay the fuck out of it."

CHAPTER 4

ZANDER

The coffee shop isn't even close to maximum capacity right now, but there are a few people at the booths and tables. A couple more lined up at the counter. My brother waits for me in one of the booths. His starched dress shirt is stretched tight across his shoulders. The privacy here is nominal. More than we'd have at one of the tables in the middle of the floor. Far less than we'd have at the motel or at the office. He's chosen a public place for a reason.

For the best, I think. Throughout our lives we've had knockdown-dragout screaming matches a few times. Siblings will do that. This can't be one of those times.

The meeting yesterday ended with Cade refusing to agree to any terms. He needed to speak to his lawyer first.

A coffee grinder whines as I approach the booth and sit down across from Cade, the guilt taking a seat alongside me. Two coffees are already on the table, both black, and Cade stares down at his like it might give him some answers if he looks long enough. His jaw is tight, eyes dark. He's obviously upset. He only glances up from the coffee cup when I reach for my own.

Fuck, I wish it hadn't come to this. If I could go back, though, what could I possibly change?

And then my gut freezes. There's concern in his hazel eyes, but he's made up his mind about something. Cade has spent a long time mastering himself. He's not one to let things slip. So even showing me this concern means this conversation has a real weight to it. I can feel it pressing down on me.

Cade looks away, back down into his coffee. "What the hell are you doing, Zander?"

I'm good at sitting still, but the urge to fidget is strong. It's because I don't have the words to explain myself. How could he possibly understand? I don't feel like we have a shared language anymore. It shouldn't be possible for the two of us to have drifted so far apart, given that we work together. But it happened.

My brother's frown deepens as he looks back at me. "You know how vulnerable she is. And you don't want to admit it, but what happened with Quincy fucked you up. It made you susceptible to this kind of thing."

Rage flares in me, followed by the pang of a deep, old guilt. Not because I felt for Quincy the way I feel for Ella. It's because the mention of her name makes every failure seem worse. All my worst moments stem from that one.

"Don't talk about her."

Cade narrows his eyes. "It's true."

My voice is low, the words coming from deep down in my chest and murmured with an edge to them that could kill. "I said, don't talk about her. Quincy doesn't have a damn thing to do with Ella, and you're not going to sit here in this fucking coffee shop and talk to me about things you know nothing about."

"Fine," snaps Cade and then he takes several deep breaths in a row. His hands flex on the table before he grips his mug again. When next he speaks his voice is level. "I asked you here to tell you that I'm letting you go from The Firm."

Cold shock washes over me. I can't believe Cade would do this. Part of me is stunned that my own brother would turn on me. It doesn't matter that I went against him first.

"You can't be serious." Stress keeps my voice tight. He isn't even man enough to look me in the eye.

His jaw works as he grits his teeth. "If you're going to be with her, you sure as hell can't be on payroll."

A tic in my jaw spasms with agreement. He's right. I have no qualms about that. My relationship with Ella will be strictly what we decide tonight. As I sit here, it all unravels in front of me, a chill running through my blood. It's not about what I want and what could be. It's only about what she needs right now. A Dominant/submissive relationship. She has to know that's all it is at the moment. I haven't forgotten our night together and her emotional response. I can care for her in only some ways. She has to accept that. Until the situation is different, that's all we can be. It's not about what I want, it's about what she needs.

My mind wanders to what I wish we could be, if things were different, until Cade stares back at me, expecting a response.

"I can't be on payroll with the company or for this case?"

"I haven't decided yet." Fresh anger flares in his eyes. "You don't understand what almost happened, Zander. If Kamden had gone to the judge rather than me, you would be in a fucking jail cell, and she would be back at the Rockford Center."

"It wasn't me who—"

"Is that what you want? Ella back at that place, isolated from everyone? Is that what you want for her?"

For her hits me like a bullet straight through the chest. It rattles around my heart and exits out the other side. Cade understands this, at least. I don't want those things. I don't want the Rockford Center for Ella. I don't want her to shrink back into that pale, silent woman.

"No." It untwists something in my chest to say it. It feels honest, and right, even if I'm completely fucked. "I don't want that for her. I did what I could to be careful."

"Bullshit." Cade's grip tightens around his coffee cup. "If you had come to me, if you had informed us, we could have adjusted. You should have waited. You should have told me."

"You're full of shit." My snide response is louder than I'd like and rewards us with an onlooker's gaze. Clearing my throat, I adjust my tone. "Ella doesn't just want what I give to her. She needs it. There's no adjusting for that. It was what brought her out of her pain enough to even talk to the rest of you."

Cade's eyes meet mine and I have the impression he's looking right through me as though he'll refuse any evidence. Like the truth doesn't matter.

"And what about you, Zander? Do you *need* it?"

Something balls up in my throat, and I can't answer him. He must see the reality in my eyes, though, because he lets out a heavy sigh. Like I've disappointed him.

Cade raises his eyes from his coffee. He's not only disapproving now, not only disappointed. He's worried about me. The instinct grows to brush it off. No one needs to worry about me. But that's not true. I wouldn't have survived after Quincy if it weren't for Damon. Fuck, I don't want to be brought back to that moment. To a place that only offers emptiness or regret. There's nothing else but that.

In some ways, I feel like that now. Everything is fucked. The ground isn't steady, and I need things. It feels unreasonable to want reassurance. I'm the one who's supposed to reassure other people, not the other way around.

It's one simple fact that gives me doubt: they could take her at any moment. There's not a damn thing I could do. The heaviness of that reality is bitter and palpable. I have to be careful, not because of her, but because of them.

I don't say this to my brother. I don't say a word because I'm too damn afraid that if I say the wrong thing, he'll convince me I shouldn't be with Ella. He's right, I do need her. I need her more than I'd like to admit.

He pushes his coffee cup aside and stands. "I have paperwork to do."

My pulse flares in my neck as I flex my hands back into fists. "And Ella?"

He looks down at me, shrugging his suit jacket back into place, and he's hovering somewhere between Cade, owner of The Firm, and Cade, my brother. There's no way to know which version will win out. "If you want to see Ella, go to her. It will not be as an employee of this company. I can't risk it."

My next breath comes easy and the change in my brother's expression tells me he knows how much relief I must feel. My hands are a breath away from shaking. I curl one into a fist on the table, and hold my coffee cup in the other. "Understandable, and I respect that decision."

"That means you'll no longer have the motel paid for."

I don't give a damn about the motel or money. "Also

understandable."

"Consider yourself on unpaid leave."

All I can do is nod. For the first time in a long time, I want to stand up and crush him in a quick embrace. He doesn't know what he's given me with this. Or maybe he does. I can't say.

Cade shifts his weight from one foot to the other, about to leave, but then he hesitates. He lets out a breath. "You need to be careful, Zander. You and Ella—you're both in positions to be hurt badly in this. Her more than you. I don't want this to end badly. So if you can walk away, I think you should."

I don't want to hug him anymore. My gratefulness shrinks until it's a more appropriate size. "That's your opinion."

"It is." He's insistent now. Like he knew that it would piss me off to make the comment, but he had to make it anyway. Cade has never shied away from having hard conversations. Sometimes he's taken it too far. I didn't expect him to become a different person over this, and he hasn't. "It is my opinion. But it's because I don't want to see anyone else hurt." He turns to go. "I'll be in contact," he says over his shoulder.

"Anyone else" is another reference to Quincy. With his back to me, he walks out of the shop, the bell above the door chiming as he goes. Leave it to Cade to get that shot in at the last moment. It all starts with her, doesn't it?

But no—no. I take a four-count breath, then another, and sit with the pain in my chest and the surge of guilt. Quincy didn't die because of me. She died because some desperate bastard with a cruel streak mugged her and killed her. What's arguable is whether I should have insisted on walking her home. I should have insisted on seeing her to a safe place, and I didn't. I allowed her to walk away.

I'm not doing that with Ella. I didn't drive back to the motel and head out of town. I didn't take no for an answer when Damon tried to keep me from her. I didn't do a damn thing until I'd spoken to her.

I want to speak to her now.

I want to do more than speak to her. I want to be back in that bedroom with the door shut and kiss her until she moans. I want to feel her body underneath mine. I want to hear the way she whispers my name in her ear.

I reach for the phone in my pocket and pull back at the last minute. That phone belongs to The Firm. There's another one snugged beside it. Mine.

I let my mind wander to her. Her soft skin. Her pouty lips. Her wide, dark eyes. Her trust.

It takes no time at all to pull up her number. To see her name on the screen. She hasn't messaged. I haven't messaged her either, even though we're both aware there's plenty to discuss. It feels as though we're just getting started. It's thrilling, but in a way that's filled with uncertainty.

Be ready for me tonight. I have a few things to work out, then I'll be over like I promised.

There's a slight pause, and then she replies.

Zander?

A smirk pulls my lips up, realizing she didn't have this number. *Yes. This is my number now. Use it as often as you'd like.*

I will. Not another second passes before she tells me, *I miss you.*

It's hard to read her tone from a text message, but I imagine it's soft. Open. She's telling me something in honesty. In more of that trust I've come to crave.

I missed her too.

CHAPTER 5

ELLA

Emotional days suck the life out of you. I don't know how or why, but it's like they eat up all of your energy, leaving you exhausted, yet you've done nothing but drown in the thoughts of your own mind. Ever since this morning, since I asked Kamden and Damon for space, I've stared at my phone and wished it was my old one.

I want to listen to James's voice message I listened to on repeat a year and a half ago. I want to tell my friends I miss him and hear them tell me they miss him too. All of my pictures, all of our conversations. It hit me harder than I thought it would bringing up what happened during that meeting. Every day, I know he died. Every day, I know I tried to kill myself because I didn't want to be alone anymore and

I felt so damn alone. It was like the world went dark and the only light I could see was by ending it. It happened quickly, yet slowly just the same. I didn't realize I'd fallen down that path until it was the only one. Everything else vanished and it was all I had left. It was my only escape from grief.

It's a ball in a box. Grief really is an unforgiving ball in a stupid little box.

I stare back down at my phone as I sniffle and wish I could take that text and send it to James. *I miss you.*

Is it wrong that I miss them both? I can tell one and he chooses not to respond. But I can't even tell the other. My first love. The man I thought I was going to spend my life with.

I'm busy pulling the sheet up to my neck, its pristine white silky fabric not coming anywhere near my eyes in case my mascara is smudged when there's a knock at the door.

The shock comes with the knowledge that it's been so long since anyone has asked permission to enter.

"Come in," I answer calmly, lifting myself to sit up on my bed, glancing in the vanity mirror. I meant to change before Zander came, but time has flown by. The silk cuffs of my pajamas are proof I lost it earlier, and I find myself cupping my hands over the bits tainted with black mascara to cover them as he enters.

The door opens slowly, creaking as it does. Zander's steps are measured and he takes his time, closing the door. My heart does a pitter-patter as if a prince has come to kiss my sleeping lips and bring me back to life. What a handsome knight in shining armor he is.

He wears a devilish smirk as his gaze roams down my body. Every inch he takes in blazes with a desperate need to be touched by this man.

Zander Thompson is sin in all black. Black jeans that hug his ass and are faded just slightly, and a black Henley is stretched tight across his broad shoulders.

Then his eyes meet mine and he tilts his head ever so slightly. His expression, though ... the seriousness can't hide the desire in his gaze.

"There are things we're going to discuss before I fuck you," he says and his deep voice barely comes out above a murmur, yet I hear every word crystal clear.

Suddenly I'm not so tired. Suddenly I'm not so sad.

I'm needy, though. I've never felt so needy in my entire life as I do now.

The floorboards groan as he shifts his weight.

I can't explain why I suddenly feel like I've done something wrong. "What do we need to talk about?"

"Your punishment." He speaks easily, slowly pacing around the bedroom. Zander loosens his collar first, giving me a perfect view of the masculine sweep of his neck.

Inching backward to rest against the headboard, I'm hesitant to ask, "What exactly do I need to be punished for?"

With his lips pulled into an asymmetric smirk, his deep

voice rumbles, "If you don't know, then maybe I should reconsider this arrangement."

"Extortion … threatening The Firm?" I say and can barely breathe, not knowing how he'll react now that we're alone. I've wanted to be at his mercy since he whispered the forbidden word, submission … and now we find ourselves here. It's difficult to maintain eye contact until he says, "That would be it, my little jailbird."

I can't help but to simper at the twist to my nickname.

His approval brings warmth and comfort, although I'm still unsure what's to come. "There's that smile I've been missing."

I could tell him how much I've missed him. How much I don't want him to leave now that he's here. Instead he speaks before my courage comes and says, "We need to decide exactly how I'll be punishing you."

My heart races from how deadly low his tone is. The leather of Zander's belt glides easily from his belt loops as he unbuckles and removes it. All the while his eyes stay on mine.

The pounding of adrenaline in my blood causes it to heat and I swear I feel that pulse between my thighs the most.

With the belt folded in his hand, he turns his back to me before dragging the lone chair from my vanity to the end of the bed, placing it there and taking a seat.

He's far too large for the dainty thing. His brooding stature takes it over.

"I apologize," I say, answering him the only way I know how.

"Good girl," he whispers with a sexed-up grin.

"Edging is what I would typically do in this situation, but—"

"Edging?"

"Orgasm denial for a few hours," he says and leans back, more casual than he was a moment ago. His thumb runs down the stubble of his jaw as he adds, "Until I'm satisfied you've been punished."

Heat simmers along my skin with the threat. James did that before. It wasn't for hours and I cussed him out during. I vaguely remember being on the verge of tears when he finally let me get mine, then he fucked me into the mattress while telling me how much he loved me.

With my heart in my throat, I whisper, "It's what you would do normally ... but?"

"But I found what you did made me hard as fuck, so I'll be rewarding you instead."

The blush that rises through me, from the tips of my toes all the way up to the crown of my head, is heated and proof I'm eager for more.

"There's—" I hesitate, my knuckles going white as I stare down at them, biting my tongue.

"Say it," Zander's voice is calm but I still can't bring myself to look up at him, the memory that begged to be spoken playing in my mind.

"Tell me right now." His tone is hardened and my gaze

whips to his.

"I don't love the pain." I whisper the confession before swallowing.

His emerald and amber gaze is assessing, and the concern in his expression is apparent with the wrinkles that form around his eyes and his downturned lips.

Swallowing thickly I add, "James had a friend once." It's only once his name is spoken that I realize how easily I've mentioned my late husband. My lover. The only man who I've given everything to. It doesn't feel like the betrayal I imagined it would. It feels like he's given me permission. Like I'm supposed to tell Zander.

"When we were playing and learning things ... he had a friend who asked questions. Most of them I didn't really pay attention to." That night was exceptional and a sigh leaves me at the memory, but the warmth that leaves means a chill settles inside of me. Picking at an imperceptible loose thread on the sheet, I peek up at Zander. "We were learning punishments and when James said I was a brat, that I pushed him to be punished, his friend asked if I loved the pain." Shaking my head comes without conscious consent. "I don't like it ... not like his submissive did."

Since Zander's come in and seated himself in the chair in front of me, the sun has begun to set and the warm hues seep into the curtains behind him. With the light dimmed, shadows play along his sharp features.

He nods once before commanding me, "Strip. Down to nothing."

I don't expect the embarrassment. With my fingers fumbling at the hem of my silk pajamas, I can't even look him in the eyes. Of everything I thought I would feel confiding in Zander, embarrassment isn't one of them. It's quickly relieved when he tells me, "I'm not a sadist, Ella. I don't love the pain either and I already knew you weren't a masochist."

My heart thuds in a way that denies the space between us, like it doesn't exist. A different kind of heat takes over as he stares into my gaze, unbuttoning his shirt with one hand and tells me, "I want you naked with your heels on the mattress, legs bent and spread, so I can taste you."

With trembling hands I comply to his every wish, not sure if this is the punishment, the reward, or some kind of concoction of the two of them swirled together.

My hair cascades and spreads like a halo around me, my chest rising and falling as I stare above at the chandelier. At the details of the natural, untreated wood and the elegant curves of the iron that shape the sphere.

My eyes only close when the bed dips and groans, and then the warmth of Zander's breath tickles my inner thigh. With his lips pressed against my skin I feel him smile as I shiver.

Looking down my body, I watch as he leaves an open mouthed kiss, teasing me. With one hand, he holds my hip, and with the other, he reaches up and plucks a nipple between his pointer and thumb. Almost carelessly, even though the sensation is directly linked to my clit.

The breath of a moan he elicits only makes me hotter. He nips at my thigh, not hard but enough that my body bucks in response. He doesn't keep me steady; he could have held me down and we both know it.

"You need to keep still," he warns, his eyes darkening. There's a heat that resonates between us, ignited from the intensity in his gaze. I only nod, barely breathing, until he catches my nipple between his fingers, rolling it. The sensation is hot yet there's a pain that comes with it.

I moan my agreement, telling him, "I'll keep still." He releases me instantly, and doesn't hesitate to drop his tongue to my slit. Taking a languid lick, he groans deep from within his chest. The rumble brings a vibration that carries to his lips.

My head falls back and I let my eyes close, focused on keeping myself still. My fingernails dig into the sheets, scratching as I tighten my grip. I want nothing more than to run them through his hair, to keep him still instead of me, to rock myself against his tongue.

A gasp escapes and I'm forced to look down at him as his tongue dives into my heat. He drags himself back up and then sucks my clit. My lips form a perfect O and I can't breathe as he causes a heat to dance along every nerve ending in my body. I'm cold all at once, my body refusing to move until the fire engulfs me and a cry of pleasure is torn from me. My back bows slightly, my shoulders digging into the mattress.

The pool of pleasure deep in my belly spreads slowly, outward and toward my limbs. His next statement catches me off guard. It's the demand, the threat that lies there when he says, "Keep your ass down or I'll tie you down."

I don't have a moment to respond before he presses his thumb against my throbbing clit, mercilessly rubbing as two of his thick fingers enter me.

With my teeth clenched, I force out profanity as he fucks me, his fingers curled so every stroke hits the wall where that bundle of sensitive nerves lies. He's relentless, near brutal as goosebumps spread along my skin.

It's beyond impossible to stay still. My legs tremble and before I can get out an apology or an excuse, Zander keeps me trapped in his gaze as he plants a kiss on my quivering thigh.

It takes everything I have to remain motionless and obey. My body begs to buck as the pleasure builds. It carries me higher and higher and I whisper, as if the single letter is a plea, "Z."

Adding in a third, he finger fucks me harder and without any mercy.

"Fuck!" I cry out, my body instinctively attempting to escape the threat of my impending climax.

It hits me just as Zander squeezes my breast. He's not gentle and the hint of pain only adds to the overwhelming pleasure. A cold sweat covers my body as the waves run through me.

My inhale is staggered as I attempt to retake my place and then I'm paralyzed by his next action.

He works his fourth finger in me, stretching me with a sweet, stinging pain. The pleasure lingers and feels especially present between my legs where it's far more tender.

"Good girl, taking what I give you." His groan of approval brings more heat. "I want to give you more."

"More?" I can barely breathe at hearing the word, already overwhelmed and stretched and full.

"Be a good girl, Ella. I want to see how much you can take." He plants a small kiss just beneath my belly button.

His fist? "Are you—fuck!" My neck arches as I scream out, loving the mix of pleasure and pain and feeling this … taken.

He doesn't look me in the eye. Instead he leans down, his broad shoulders forcing my legs farther apart. He takes my clit into his mouth, sucking harder than he did before and my head drops as the sounds of him working his hand promise me that the reality is exactly what I think it is. His fingers bend, his knuckles brutally pushing against my walls, his pace never lessening.

It's all too much. I'm too hot, the pleasure building again, far more this time, taking me higher, to a place where I know the fall will destroy me after it's taken me.

My throat feels raw, the safe word hovering, threatening to be spoken. I feel full, tight, ready to split. A shiver rides up my shoulders just as I feel him press the tip of his thumb in and I can't take it.

I can't take any more. I'm so close once again. Too close. Too full.

"It's too much," I try to speak, but the words are incoherent. "Pink. Pink," I say and struggle, my head pressed firmly to the pillow, my body still shaking. All at once, I'm empty and cold.

"I've got you." Zander's voice is steadying as I roll onto my side. My legs collapse together and the blanket is pulled around my shoulders, the warmth nothing compared to what Z had just done to me. My shoulders shake with a shiver that's only subdued when my Dominant lies behind me, his chest to my back, his arms around me, holding me tightly.

I didn't even feel the tears that had leaked out of the corner of my eyes and rolled down my cheeks until my heart stopped hammering.

"I've got you," he whispers, his lips at the shell of my ear. He shushes me, he tells me it's all right.

I'm barely cognizant of what just happened. When my breathing calms, I realize I safe worded. "I didn't mean to."

My denial is met with a kiss on the curve of my neck. Not too short, an openmouthed version that lingers. "You did," he says. With his lips in my hair, he kisses me again. His arm tightens, pulling me to him as he tells me it's all right.

I recall only safe wording once with James. Only when he cracked the whip and it broke my skin. Only once because of the sudden pain and fear. I was terrified. That was an entirely different experience. He apologized. He held me, but I was crying. The pain lasted and I shoved him away. It was awful.

This … this doesn't feel like that at all. Not in the least.

"You're crying." Zander's voice is full of concern. I wish I could say anything, but I can't utter a word.

"Where do you hurt?"

I can't answer his question because it's not like he could do a damn thing to fix it. Damon said I may be displacing my feelings and I think he might be right. I still love James. I love him and I think I love Zander too, but I don't know how that's possible.

"It's okay, you can cry." I know he's looking down at me but I keep my eyes shut tight. "If you want me to stop—"

"Don't stop." I beg him with quickly ushered words. "Don't stop. Please, Z, hold me."

CHAPTER 6

ZANDER

Scrolling through the photos on Ella's various social media accounts leaves a longing to know who this beautiful woman used to be. She hasn't posted regularly in nearly two years now but I scroll past flirtatious grins and obvious laughter, past a woman celebrating life and exuding strength with a no-fucks-given attitude. There are pictures of him as well. Her sneaking up on him and laying with him on sunny tropical beaches. Pictures of him kissing her and where she's kissing him. There's an obvious point where her public persona was tamed. Just prior to their wedding photos, she appears wild and free. And then it changes, to bright smiles and "love and light" captions.

There are wholesome posts about her charity work, but it

doesn't take much to be certain that prior to marrying James, Ella was known for her partying.

The fireplace in Ella's sitting room is off, adding to the quiet. The blue of the paint is suffused with gray light from the early morning. She's still sleeping upstairs, leaving me alone in the chill of this room.

I came here out of habit. I didn't know what to do with myself when I woke up in her bed. I found a spare toothbrush in the bathroom, still wrapped in plastic among other travel-sized toiletries. She was sleeping so deeply when I finally let go of her that I couldn't bear to wake her. I tugged her blanket up to her shoulders and quietly slipped out to the room that's most familiar to me. We've spent the most time here, in the blue sitting room. And in its silence, I've let my mind wander, I've let the questions repeat themself over and over. *Am I doing the right thing? Is this really what's best for her?*

I'm only her Dom, so there's no reason for me to be here. Not technically. It's storming outside and I watch the raindrops fall against the window. When the wind blows, it's vicious, battering the small droplets against the panes. Unless we're going to have a true 24/7 relationship, then I can't be here all the time.

Even if a part of me wanted to be here, simply because she's most comfortable here, a much larger part of me doesn't want to develop this relationship anywhere other than my own home.

We're going to have to talk about it, and soon. This is a crucial boundary between the two of us. When I'll come over, and how long I'll stay. I need to make clear to her that she was only agreeing to the relationship we had before, nothing else. I'll help her as her Dom. Although I would never make this arrangement with anyone else who couldn't leave the confines of their home. With the only other 24/7 power exchange relationship I've had, the only true D/s relationship, she lived with me. *Quincy.*

Quincy, who has been the subject of at least one phone call this morning. A phone call I let go to voicemail. The hearing's coming up, and I don't want to talk about it.

A larger sheet of rain sweeps across the yard and taps more forcefully against the windowpane. I've never lived in a place like this, with all this space.

All this wealth.

Across the house, the front door opens. I hear it click shut quietly. It's far too early for Silas to switch off with Damon. The footsteps and the jingle of keys is telling. I stay where I am, my jaw clenching slightly. He can come to me.

Kamden appears in the sitting room doorway with my temper barely contained, the anger still palpable. The air between us seems thick. Weighted. He narrows his eyes and watches me from the opening, then straightens up and strides in, taking the seat across from me. He's exaggerated about it. Casual. But it's not casual, and we both know it.

From the tight set of his jaw I think he might like to hit me. The very idea begs my lips to pull up into a smirk, but I keep my expression neutral.

It seems we feel the same about one another.

He lets the silence stretch out, and so do I. I've thought about what I'd say to him, but every conversation is different as I play it out. More importantly, I need to be careful. He's Ella's conservator. There is far too much at risk for her to allow my ego to take center stage.

Everything outside of the two of us, is a risk. She isn't in charge of her own decisions. I don't have authority in that aspect of her life either. Pissing off the wrong person could end in me not having access to her at all. Had I not been able to convince Cade and Kamden, things could be very different right now. The Firm, Kamden, even her closest friends. One wrong step and we could be buried in problems I don't know how to get out of.

Wind rushes outside the window now. The rain lets up a little, then comes back down hard. It's one of those fall storms that steals the warmth from the air and makes it feel frigid afterward, even if snow is weeks from falling. The heat kicks on in Ella's house, with the faintest of clicks. Other than the leather groaning beneath Kamden as he readjusts to lean forward, his elbows on his knees, it's the only sound in the room. But not for long.

"If you hurt her, I will destroy you," Kamden says beneath

his breath.

I stare at him across the space between us. "That a threat, Kam?" A heat travels up my spine and across my shoulders. Instinctively, my fingers curl slightly, ready to ball into fists.

"It's a promise." His voice is clear, raised so there's no doubt I can hear. "You wouldn't be the first man who thought he could use her."

A crease forms between my brows as my eyes narrow at him. That's fucking rich, coming from the man who installed cameras in her home to spy on her. Fucking rich. Every ounce of anger calls at the back of my throat. Keeping a stone-cold expression I'm careful with my response, knowing full well the power he has over her. I've never hated a soul more than him.

"I'm not using Ella."

"Of course you are." His statement comes with a sadness he fails to contain. If I'm not mistaken, a fear as well. He stares into the empty fireplace, refusing to look back at me. "Even if you don't want to admit it. You're using her."

"You'd know that from experience, right?"

"Fuck you," Kamden spits, his eyes coming back to mine. I've pissed him off enough with that one remark to make color come to his cheeks. "You don't know what the hell you're talking about. She's like my little sister."

I want to call him out on the cameras. Even if Ella were Kamden's little sister, he sure as hell shouldn't have been putting up cameras without asking her. But a guy like

Kamden will have come up with a justification for himself. One that I won't be able to change, or counter.

Besides. There are other things I know about Kamden.

"She's like your little sister, but you didn't go to visit her." My tone is deathly low, and wrought with emotion I didn't realize I had for that small fact. I don't bother to hide it, the obvious pain he caused her. "She was alone, locked away, and you didn't visit her once."

All that color runs out of his cheeks, leaving him strangely pale in the gray light coming through the window. Ella told me he never went to visit her while she was at the Rockford Center, and that is definitely the kind of thing an older brother type would do. It's most certainly the kind of thing Kamden should have done.

Kamden opens his mouth. "I—" A subtle shake of his head stops him from continuing. He was going to tell me one thing, and then he changed his mind. His thumbnail finding his bottom teeth as he leans back, once again he focuses on the empty fire. Another few long seconds go by. The rain makes it easier to sit through this conversation. It gives me something to listen to other than the beat of my heart and all my own thoughts. His expression gives me something new to think about; it reads nothing but regret. The longer I sit, the more questions build in my mind.

"I had a relapse," he admits in a whisper and then clears his throat, meeting my eyes. "I didn't go to see her, because

I couldn't. I know one of your dirty secrets. Now you know one of mine."

"A relapse?" The leather armrest tightens under my grasp. Kamden stands up and shrugs off his jacket. He's wearing a heather gray shirt underneath with his jeans. He'd look comfortable here if he weren't trying to suppress so much emotion. He tosses the jacket onto one of the other chairs and sits down again.

"I overdosed." Kamden's mouth curves down, his cheeks reddening again, and I'd know that expression anywhere. I've seen it on my own face in the mirror enough times. He settles back into the chair and he's joined by guilt.

Guilt. Real, pained guilt.

That heat I felt before dims instead as I watch him, finding no trace of deception.

Kamden clears his throat. "Fuck you for judging me." His eyes are hard on mine now. He looks like this hurts to say even more than admitting the relapse. "I found her. I'm the one who found her. She'd jumped out of a window. Not this place. I can't go back to her southern home. I thought she was dead. Lying there like a corpse, there was so much blood by her head. I thought she was dead."

The image slams into me like a long-haul truck. Ella, lying lifeless and still on the ground outside some featureless window. The horrified feeling of coming upon her that way. The slow realization. Kamden wouldn't have wanted to believe it was true. Reality would have forced its way in anyway. She had lived. Obviously she had lived. But there would have been a moment when his heart was in his throat, when his mind was screaming for her not to have done what she did. My own heart pounds to imagine it. I have to keep my face neutral with every bit of restraint I have.

It's far more serious than I thought with Ella. I thought she had a moment of weakness once. Only once. "She tried to kill herself more than once?"

"Twice now," Kamden answers and swallows hard. "She was admitted after she jumped out the window. The only thing that saved her that time was the railing. Her ankle caught it on the way down and prevented her from landing on concrete stairs." He readjusts again in his seat, this time opting to sit back, his gaze focusing on the blanket. Like all he wants to do is hide beneath it. As if it could all be written off as a bad dream. "I couldn't do anything about it. The police came. I was in shock. She'd jumped. It was obvious. I wasn't there when they spoke to her when she woke up, they wouldn't let me. They admitted her before I could do a damn thing to help her."

A chill settles between us, dragging the tension down to the ground until it's subdued entirely. All I can wonder is if Damon knows. My mind drifts to the file. Kamden's quiet for another long stretch until he tells me, "And then, at the center, she drank drain cleaner. I've been—" He stops, putting a fist to his mouth, and takes a deep breath. Putting his hands in his lap before he continues. "I've been clean for a decade, but I couldn't stop blaming myself."

"For what? What did you do?"

"I'm the one who left her alone in the first place." His eyes find mine. "She was losing it. Crying, which I expected. But she was angry and hysterical."

This wouldn't have been in the file. Even if I'd read it, this statement from Kamden wouldn't have been in there. He wouldn't be telling me now if he assumed I already knew about it. It comes back to me then—Ella telling me that everything in the file was carefully curated. I thought she meant she did it all by herself, but Kamden must have had a hand too. He must have kept out certain details.

"You left her alone because she was upset?" I shake my head, my own guilt rising again. I did the same thing. I let Quincy walk through the city by herself. I want to convince Kamden it wasn't his fault as much as I want to convince myself, but lies don't help a damn soul.

"No. I left her alone, and I took her phone. So she had no one. I took her phone," he repeats as if the phone is what did her in. "She couldn't call anyone ... but she couldn't have it. It was driving her mad."

None of this makes any sense. "Why the hell would you take her phone?"

He's looking into the fireplace again, and I almost wish

I'd turned the damn thing on so he wouldn't look so desolate while he stares into nothing. Kamden takes a trip back into his memories and resurfaces with a shake of his head. "They kept posting it. The video. It was all over her social. They kept tagging her, over and over again. Every time she saw one pop up, she lost it."

"Posting the video?"

"Ella kept watching it over and over. Someone would tag her and the whole cycle would start again. She couldn't stop herself. She'd play the video and cry. Gut-wrenching sobs. All day. After a few hours she'd manage to collect herself, but it would only be for a few minutes. An hour at most. And then she went back to the video. Back and back and back. When it was at its worst she would beg people to stop posting, but they wouldn't. Asking them to take it down only made more people share the link. It was vicious. She had nowhere to go. Maybe you don't get it, but sharing everything with them ... she couldn't back away and they wouldn't let her."

I'm missing a crucial piece of information, and for the first time I feel a real, genuine regret that I haven't read her file. I haven't done everything in my power to learn about Ella. I'm against it in general because I think people need the chance to tell their own stories, but this is a part of it that she's yet to confide in me.

I didn't know about the suicide attempt at her old place. I didn't know she jumped out of a fucking window. And

Kamden thinks she did that because of some people posting about her. No—posting a video. I've seen some videos, but—

"What were they posting?"

Kamden meets my eyes with deep disappointment. Somehow, the tables have turned since he walked into this room. "You want to make me the villain in all this because you're pissed off at me, but I'm not the villain. You might be, though."

"What got to her—" I stop and take a deep breath. I won't let my anger get the best of me. I won't even talk myself up into thinking I haven't made any mistakes. "What did they post that made her that upset?" It has to do with James. It's the only thing I can imagine. The realization is suffocating.

Kamden looks down at his hands in his lap, then back up to me. "You should ask her." He shakes his head then adds, "No. You should already know."

CHAPTER 7

ELLA

I haven't looked forward to Damon and his chats. It's something I've tolerated because I was told I had to do it. Therapy isn't something I've ever wanted. Until this morning.

Waking up to find another gift from Kam, glazed pastries from a quaint French bakery downtown, and a note from Zander, letting me know he had to have arrangements made but would see me tonight ... left me feeling more alone than I'd have liked. Barefoot in the kitchen, that sinking feeling resonated until Damon walked into the room.

"Is there anything you want to talk about this morning?" Damon's professional as always, but I don't miss his subtle change in expression when he glances down at my nightgown. It's the same one from yesterday. I was eager to get downstairs, to find Zander and didn't think much else of, well, of anything else.

"Aren't you the one who's supposed to pick those topics?"

"I could ... just thought I'd offer," he says and shrugs. Eyeing him I wonder how this man always looks so professional. Even in only a simple white tee and faded blue jeans, he radiates an aura of strength. Freshly shaven, his dark skin taut over his muscular arms. It's easy to decide that it's just him. It's the air around him. Everything about him reads: authority.

And then there's me. In a wrinkled nightshirt, with finger-combed hair.

Clearing my throat, I hesitantly take a seat at the counter. "I haven't brushed my teeth, let alone begun to think about what we should talk about." Lies. The softly spoken words sound like lies even to my own ears.

"There's nothing you want to talk about?" he questions. Staring past him to the kettle still on the stove from yesterday, I wonder if Z told him about last night. I wouldn't think so, but then again, I'm not a part of those conversations. There's so much out of my own control.

"You seem ..."

"Out of it?" I surmise.

"Upset," he says, correcting me. The stool grates on the floor as I stand up and busy myself with the kettle.

In truth, I'm exhausted. I slept so well, yet it feels like

I haven't slept at all. With the water running he questions, "Are you all right?"

With a gentle sigh escaping, I tell him, "I'll be all right. Just feeling needy today."

Damon nods, rounding the counter to join me in the working space of the kitchen. He manhandles the coffee pot, finding it empty.

When he opens the canister, the scent of fresh grounds filling the room, I comment on how much I love the smell.

Which he duly ignores. "Is there anything in particular that upset you this morning?" Even though he's facing a now brewing pot of coffee, pretending like he's not watching me, I feel his eyes on the side of my face. That's when I realize I'm watching a kettle, waiting for the pot to boil.

"It's just a ball in a box," I murmur, knowing full well why I'm upset. "I'm still grieving."

Damon's charming smile isn't what I expect to see from him. He nods and says, "We always grieve."

I nod in return and debate on letting it all out. Telling him about last night, but maybe he already knows.

"Did Z tell you?" I whisper the question.

Grabbing his mug of black coffee with both hands, he shakes his head. "Did something happen?"

I scoot from in front of the stove to the counter so I can rest my back against it, gripping the edge on either side. "Last night, I just ... I had a moment."

Damon gestures to the breakfast nook to the right with his mug. "Would you like to sit?"

Raising a brow, I ask him, "Would you like to add your sugar and cream?" My sarcastic response grants me an even broader smile. "Sitting can wait until I at least have a cup of tea," I add as he sets his mug down and adds cream and sugar as he always does.

"You know there isn't a story worth not having sugar in your morning brew."

The spoon stops mid-twirl in his mug at my comment, the warmth leaving his expression for a moment as he seems to carefully consider his words. "There is purpose in suffering."

"What?"

"I wanted to wait for the right time, but I feel like you need to know that this morning."

He peeks at me from the corner of his eye as the kettle whistles.

"There is purpose in suffering." He leans against the counter as I prepare my tea. "It wasn't so much that I was caught up in your story, not that I wasn't invested." He adds, "Just ... more that I wanted to make sure I told you that."

"Mr. Dwell-in-your-emotions thinks there's purpose in suffering ... how am I not surprised by that?" I offer wryly but with a semblance of a smirk.

He takes his time, his heavy footsteps careful as he takes a seat at the small table. After a moment, I join him, letting the tea steep and watching the steam billow.

Since Zander didn't tell Damon, I don't want to confess that I cried last night. But I wanted to get these thoughts out of me. I need someone else to take them. "I don't often feel scared. But I do now. It's alarming how scared I am."

"Why do you say that?"

"At one point in my life I had so much to lose, and yet, there wasn't much at all that I was afraid of."

Speaking the words out loud makes so much of it real. I'm scared. Maybe I'm just as scared as I am upset.

"There was a time that I was scared to be hated. Then someone told me if there aren't people out there who hate you, then it's because no one knows who you are. People with viewpoints are hated; my favorite people are demons in someone else's story. Don't you want to be someone who is known for what they believe in?" I recall the conversation I had, but I don't even remember who gave me the advice. "That's why I wanted it all out there. It's why I love that I got to share my life. I was hated, but everyone knew damn well what I believed in and I found the people who wanted the same in life." Peeking up at Damon I tell him, "I remember I wasn't scared anymore after that. Not like I was."

"But you're scared now?" he asks and my throat dries as I nod. I confess in a whisper, "I'm terrified."

"What are you scared of?"

"I haven't shared much in a long time."

"Kamden said you've started, though," he comments, his voice hopeful.

"Only two posts."

"It's something."

"It is."

"So you want to share more and you're scared of that."

"Not of sharing per se ... scared of not sharing where I stand. It's just ... it's complicated."

"What are you afraid of now?"

"It feels like I have so little left."

"In this big house?" he jokes in a calm, comforting way. I know he's got a smile on his face and he's watching me, but I can only watch the billowing steam.

In my silence, he presses, "Money?"

"No ... money is fine. It comes and goes, but money is fine. ... It's just there are things that I want to talk about, and I'm afraid if I share it with them ..." I can't bring myself to say it, but somehow I do. "If I share it, somehow they'll make it hurt. They'll make that little piece that means so much, become insignificant and then there won't be anything left at all."

"Well, you know no one has control over you. Only you do. You can only control yourself."

Nodding, my response is cracked when spoken. "I know."

"Maybe you should keep some things to yourself. It's not a bad thing. You don't owe anyone anything."

"It feels selfish in a way."

"Protecting yourself isn't selfish." Damon's adamant, but so is my phone that buzzes with a new text. The cement block that it is, opens to reveal a simple question.

"Everything okay?" Damon asks when I go quiet.

"It's just Kam. He wants to have a meeting soon." Toying with the phone I add, "He asked me when I'm free."

"And that upsets you?" he asks, gauging my solemn expression.

"He's never asked before." Again, that cold, lonely feeling that overwhelmed me when I woke up covers every inch of my skin.

"Things are different now." I swallow down the regret and push my phone away. "Everything is different."

"Different is not only okay. Different is good sometimes."

"I just wish some things could go back to the way they were."

"Which things?" he asks and my answer is immediate. "I wish I weren't so damn afraid."

"What are you afraid of?"

"That I'm going to make a mistake. Just one and I'm going to lose everything because of it." Zander. I'm going to lose Zander. I can't tell him, because even confessing that to Damon feels like it could lead to me losing him. No matter where I look, I think, one step, and it's all gone.

CHAPTER 8

ZANDER

There's a bite in the air when I pull up behind Ella's the next evening. Sunset comes faster in the fall, and it's almost finished now. Not quite cold enough for a winter coat, but there's a frosty edge to the breeze. The kitchen lights are on, spilling light out onto the porch, and Damon's in there.

Staring down at my phone, I see there are three unanswered messages.

Kamden: Have you talked to her? You need to really talk to her.

Cade: There's no chance in hell that she's moving out of that house. She's under our protection and to the judge's order, it is only under the condition that she stays at that location. And the cameras will be staying. I can't make exceptions and you know that.

Damon: I don't know what happened last night, but you should have been there this morning.

Everyone is watching us. Judging us. Even worse, their approval is an actual fucking factor in our relationship. None of this is ideal.

Another message comes in. This one from one of the lawyers involved in Quincy's case.

Arguments start at 9:30 sharp—wanted to keep you updated. Courtroom will be open if you want to sit in.

For a brief moment, I hesitate in the car. It would be far too easy to tell them all to fuck off. To tell them I'm handling it, that I've got her. It's their intentions that kept me from texting each one of them just that. I'll give Kamden the benefit of the doubt. They all have her best interest at heart. We all want the same thing: for Ella to be healthy and happy.

All day I've wondered what it is I want from this, and all that resonated was the moment in her kitchen when I heard her laugh for the first time. When she smiled up at me with a knowing look. I want that flirtatious look in her eyes. I want her moaning my name. I want her.

Clicking off my phone and shoving it into my back pocket, I settle on not responding until I speak to Ella and decide together what I should tell them.

Damon's message is the one that blindsided me the most. Him telling me I should have been there doesn't sit well with me. If he's pissed at me for turning my back on The Firm, he should say it.

It's not like we haven't had our differences before. If he really thinks I've fucked up with her, though ... that's a different story.

I've had enough confrontation for one day. I throw the door open and get out. My duffle is in the trunk; with the click of the key fob, it opens easily enough.

It took me all damn day to find a suitable place to rent close by, to get out of my lease, to schedule the movers and clear out the motel. If I had control like I'd prefer, she would have been beside me.

I spent half the day in the fucking car rearranging my life, and my best friend wants to give me shit over it. I know Ella needs to be cared for. I only left because I trusted him to do just that. Heaving the duffle over my shoulder, I'm more confident tonight than I was last night. I have everything we need for now. I can take it over from here, within the confines this situation allows.

I head for the door instead of dwelling on it any longer. Long, even strides. Like I belong here. Which I do. Ella wants me here, and that's all that matters. What doesn't matter is the prickling under the collar of my jacket and the way my nerves go cold. Seeing her feels so damn flimsy now that I've left The Firm.

Yes, I crossed professional boundaries with Ella. Yes, I did it over and over again. But at least when I was at The Firm I was guaranteed my nine-to-nine shift with her. I could count on it. Now it seems tenuous. One step out of place, and they could lock me out. Move her to a secure location. It's a fine, fine distinction. Any hint from her that she doesn't want me around, and they could escort me out.

It feels as if we're caged in. That's what each step feels like. Like I'm walking into a cage. The only saving grace is that she's in there with me and so long as I'm there, she'll be safe.

Staying calm for her is what anchors me to the ground. It's not a very sturdy anchor. This kind of visiting, where I don't really belong with the company and I don't really belong to Ella, makes me feel like I'm on the deck of a small ship caught in a storm. The waves seem reckless in my imagination.

My thumb runs down the sharp edge of the key, a key only given to me when I worked with The Firm. Staring at the doorknob, I focus on why I'm here.

I want her and she wants me. It's as simple as that.

The moment I open the door, the warmth greets me just as the bright light from the kitchen does. Slipping the handle of the duffle down my shoulder, I set the bag down and gently close the door.

Damon's eyes come up from his phone to meet mine from where he's sitting on a stool by the counter.

The realization I've come to is simple: there's no chance in hell for privacy here.

"You look like hell," my best friend says.

I run a hand over my head. "I have a lot on my mind."

Damon nods, then swipes his thumb over his phone screen and puts the phone in his pocket. From the way he presses his lips together I know he's got things on his mind too.

"I got your text," I tell him, dropping the bag and tossing my keys on the counter. "How is she?"

The question falls into the quiet of the kitchen. Damon huffs out a breath. This is close to how it would be if we were trading off shifts, but I'm not working with him anymore. This is a problem that will keep coming up between us until we solve it. Awkwardness tightens my chest and squeezes the air out of my lungs. Our routines are all wrapped up in The Firm. It's like pricking yourself on the same splinter at the back door of your house. Hurts every time, but until you sand down the wood, make it all right, it'll never let you rest.

His dark eyes meet mine. "I thought that after what happened, she might withdraw. Close up. I was prepared for the scenario where we'd have to start all over with her therapy and with her trust. But she opened up this morning … I think it would have benefitted her to have you here."

"Where is she?"

"Taking a shower now."

"I'm going to go over our new arrangement today." I drag out a chair at the table, taking a seat opposite him.

"What's the plan?"

"I'll stay here. Twenty-four seven power exchange. It'll be easier to be honest, now that I don't have shifts where I'm done."

"Staying here?"

I don't hide my dismay. "We don't have a choice."

Damon's gaze settles behind me by the door, where the duffle bag sits. "You really have feelings for her, don't you?" he asks.

Without my conscious consent, I answer, "Yes." My gaze drops and the pad of my thumb runs down the side of my pointer. "I have feelings for her."

Damon grins across the table and tells me, "Don't look so damn terrified."

"I question if she knows what she really wants. If I even know what I really want. Beyond what we're currently doing."

"What if what you're currently doing is enough?" he asks me.

My smirk in response lacks all humor. "We both know this is temporary." I grind my teeth together rather than adding, *I don't want to fail her.* I'm so fucking conflicted with her. Even my Dom side is holding back. She's fragile, everyone is watching and I don't know if once all of this is over that she's still going to want this. She's still mourning her husband... all of it, keeps me on edge when I think about the idea of us. But then I'm with her, and all I can do is fall.

"Who knows this is temporary? You and her?"

"You and I."

Tapping his knuckles on the table, Damon shakes his head. "I don't know that."

"If she didn't need me, I wouldn't be here, is what I'm saying."

"And when she doesn't need you—"

"Then I'll be gone." I finish the statement for him.

"And what if you become her safe place? You ever wonder that?"

"I still don't know that what I want would be enough for her."

"I think you're lying to yourself."

Rather than engage, I change the subject. "Is there anything you'd suggest I lead her toward today?" Damon cocks his head to the side and looks at me. I add, "I thought I'd spoil her tonight and we can lay out terms."

"Just one thing, be careful."

"I'm careful with her. Maybe too careful."

"Not just with her. Be careful, Zander."

CHAPTER 9

ELLA

The feeling from this morning hasn't left.

It's the comedown from the high. I fought for what I wanted, I won ... but what is it that I'm left with?

I'm still under a conservatorship. I'm still mandated to be in the confines of my home until I prove my mental stability to someone I don't even know and only when Damon, and The Firm, recommends an examination be done. I have no control over either.

And then there's Zander, a man I intend to give what little control I have left. A man who stirs up a number of feelings that I can barely categorize ... especially since Damon made that comment. It won't stop echoing in my head. Maybe I'm displacing the love I had for James onto Zander.

The leather journal with rose gold binding has two sheets filled with nothing but questions.

All I know for certain is that I don't have any answers and that I'm a far distance away from where I want to be. With all of the memories flooding me today, I long to go back more than anything else.

Back to a time before all of this was set into motion.

My phone buzzes with a text from Kelly. *You're supposed to hold it.*

My gaze shifts to the nightstand where the smoky quartz has sat since Kelly sent it in the mail.

She adds, *I swear it works.*

I don't have a single comment to make about the crystal and Kelly's hippie-dippie solution to everything. If I wasn't on medication, I imagine she'd have gifted me pot as well.

I'll hold it during my therapy sessions. My thumb hovers over the button, but before I can second-guess it, I send the message.

Perfect! She replies instantly and then asks another question about Zander. *What's his shoe size?* Her question forces a sly smile from me.

Kam must have reached out to Trish and Kelly and given them this number. All three of them have been texting me today. They've been asking about Zander and anything else ... other than the obvious. None of them have asked about what happened or how I'm doing in that respect.

The girls want to know all about him most of all. The secret love interest. If only they knew the whole truth.

I'll tell you tomorrow, I write back and Kelly replies with, *I can't wait.*

Girls' luncheons are going to be my new favorite, Trish says next.

Kelly piles on with, *Seriously, this has been missing from my life. Love you girls.*

Kisses.

Setting the phone down on the dresser, I wonder how much I should tell them. He's still a secret ... at least to most people. They think he's just a bodyguard from the private security firm I hired and I struggle with how much I should tell them.

At that thought, there's a knock at my bedroom door. He's the only one who knocks ... as if there's a semblance of privacy in this home. There are cameras everywhere. I call out while peering up at the camera in the corner of the room. It's tucked away, small and insignificant, yet it's one more indication that they're always watching.

"Come in." The door creaks open.

Damon told me Cade added motion sensors above the bedroom door. So they're alerted to anyone coming or going. He not-so-subtly hinted around the fact that when Zander and I are together here, they'll stop watching.

I'm very aware that it will still be recorded. It's odd the

sensation it gives me and how it's so strikingly different from when I'm recorded alone. One is troublesome and alarming, while the other is tantalizing.

With only the corner light on, and the evening sun filtering through the curtains, my prince is cast in shadows as he closes the door behind him.

My periwinkle silk nightgown is in complete contrast to his stiff white collared shirt and perfectly tailored slacks. All but the top button is done. It does nothing to hide his muscular physique and the power that lies under the expensive fabric.

"There you are," he comments as if he's been looking for me. I heard him come in. I heard them talking.

"You weren't here this morning," I say and the statement comes out as an accusation. There's a flash in his eyes. I know I've tested him. But it's gone as quickly as it came.

"I had a few things to take care of." He considers me and I do the same to him. His gaze roams down my body and his posture changes, his hand seeming to ache at his side as he flexes it. The door closes then with a final click and he stalks toward me, each step measured and quiet. Like a hunter to his prey.

I can't help what he does to me. How the air heats and each breath is harder to inhale.

Licking his bottom lip, he stops feet from me. My back to the mirror at my vanity, I stare back at him, noting that

I'm cornered.

"You're disappointed?" he questions, seemingly surprised with a cocked brow.

I answer him honestly. "I'm not sure what to expect."

"Tell me what you want, and I'll tell you if you can have it." He doesn't let a moment pass before answering easily. Checking over his shoulder, he decides to lean against the dresser, putting more space between us.

"Just tell you and you'll make it happen?"

"If I determine it necessary, yes." His voice lowers, as does his gaze to where the button is undone between my breasts. I'm more than aware that this nightgown leaves little to the imagination when it comes to my chest.

"I want you to be here when I wake up ... at least if we," I clear my throat, composing myself and remembering who the hell I am. "If we fucked the night before, I want to wake up beside you."

The strength in my tone raises Zander's gaze and he nods. "I will make sure that happens moving forward." I didn't realize I was holding my breath until he answers. Nodding slightly, I place my phone down on the vanity next to my hairbrush.

There's something liberating in that simplicity.

In the quiet, he rumbles, "I missed kissing you." The warmth returns with full force. My guard is crumbling; I feel every piece fall and I don't care.

"Is that all you missed?" I say, teasing him without

thinking much of it.

"Come here," he commands me in a whisper. It's easy to obey. His hand finds the small of my waist, pulling me in for a chaste kiss. It's simple, all of it is so easy and so bare. Yet I crumble and heat at his touch, feeling more vulnerable with every fraction of a second.

The feel of his kiss still pressed against my lips, my eyes closed and my blood warming, I push out the words that have wreaked havoc on my mind while he's been gone.

"Damon suggested I may be displacing some of my feelings." I push them out as quickly as I can, too scared to open my eyes until the last word is spoken.

He doesn't answer and slowly, I peek up at him through my lashes. The only movement he makes is to run his thumb up and down my side.

"What do you think?"

"I don't know. I know I feel things ... I don't know what you feel."

"You're feeling uncertain?"

"Yes."

"Mmm," he says and his acknowledgment is a rumble from his chest. He pulls me forward, into his chest, to kiss the crown of my head, then he whispers, "You still want me?"

"Yes," I answer easily, my eyes still open, staring down at his chest.

"Good," he answers and pulls back, letting cool air filter

between us to look down at me. "Even if you don't want me for forever, you damn well better know that I want you right now."

"And tomorrow?" Peeking up at him, I feel nothing but vulnerable.

"I'll want you tomorrow too. So long as you want this, I will be here."

I've never felt so needy before. So fragile with a man. James happened slowly. We were friends first and falling for him was unexpected. The security was there. By the time I realized what I felt, I knew he felt the same. This ... this is nothing like that and it's terrifying.

"I'm afraid ... you don't really want me. That you're only here because you think I need you."

Zander's inhale is audible, and it's heavy and suffocating all at once. His expression is just as alarming. It's as if the air around him has darkened and a different side of him has taken over. With a single step forward, he towers over me.

"If I didn't want you, I wouldn't be here, Ella." The disappointment is obvious in his piercing gaze. "How could you possibly think I don't want you? It's fucking embarrassing what you do to me. How I can't even think when you're around." Taking my hand in his, he presses my palm against him. "I'm hard as fuck thinking of how I'm going to punish you for that insecurity."

His touch is like fire, the air engulfed in flames around us.

"You missed being punished, didn't you? When you

opened your mouth to greet me and instead you complained."

My gaze dances between his broad chest and his hand.

"I'm sorry," I admit.

He smirks at me. "No you're not."

"I—"

"You wanted to test me. To push me. To make me prove myself." My body heats with a knowing feeling as he takes a step forward and I take one back. Then again. And again.

"It's called topping from the bottom." My lower back hits the vanity. I grip it on either side of me as Zander lowers his lips to my ear and whispers, "Did you think I'd let you get away with it?"

"Z." I swallow thickly, not knowing what to say. "I was upset and unsure. I'm sorry." It's not that I fear a damn thing in this moment. Not him leaving, not a punishment. That's not why I'm sorry. I wish I could take it back, because I know it hurt him. That flash in his eyes, that disappointment. "I would take it back if I could."

"You are my submissive, and you were disrespectful." His admonishment is spoken slowly. "Get down on your knees and show me how sorry you are."

I'm almost shocked by his disapproval, by the harshness of his tone. Shocked so much that I freeze until he lowers his lips to mine, his eyes still open, staring through me as he demands. "On your fucking knees right now. Get on the floor."

I fall instantly to my knees, my cheek brushing down

his thigh until I'm eye level with his groin. As my fingers fumble with his zipper, he pets the back of my head and then strokes my cheek with a single finger. "That's a good girl. Make it up to me."

In a single yank his cock juts up. Thick and hard, the veins running down his length and drawing my eye. I don't waste a second before licking the bead of precum from the smooth head of his dick. My tongue runs along the seam and the act makes him hiss.

I lick his length for lubricant before wrapping my hand around him. He's got enough girth that my hands are too small to fully wrap around him, so I use both, stroking him and rocking myself as I do.

"Give me that mouth of yours."

With both hands pumping the base of his cock, I wrap my mouth around his head and press my tongue along the bottom side. "Good girl. That's it." I moan around his length, sucking and feeling my own desire build. I'm hot for him.

He groans, "Goddamn," breathily which only fuels me further to please him.

Every little sound he makes, the hitches in his breathing, the deep moans—they all push me to move faster, to please him and get him off.

"Take more of me," he says, pushing himself deeper. I swallow down as much of him as I can, until I gag. Sputtering on his cock, I have to pull away.

As I heave in a breath, he grabs the back of my head. The head of his dick pushes in deeper and deeper. Arching my neck so he can take over, I let him guide himself as my hands move to the back of his thighs to steady myself and keep me upright.

Fisting the hair at the nape of my neck, he keeps me still as he thrusts himself deeper. My eyes sting as he cuts off my breathing. My nails dig into the expensive fabric of his pants.

As he pulls out, I heave in a breath, staring up at him. His jaw is clenched tight as he groans in pleasure.

"Your mouth is good for two things, my smart-ass girl," he tells me and pulls away. Leaving me breathing heavily, with a primal need that stirs a burning fire within me.

"Stay," he commands, backing away, zipping his pants although he's still very much erect.

I'm left alone on my knees on the other side of the bedroom, catching my breath as he opens the bedroom door. My lips part a moment in protest, until he comes back into view, a duffle bag in hand that he sets onto the bench at the foot of the bed.

"Tonight we're going to play," he informs me.

"I want to play."

His short laugh is nearly condescending. "I'm aware you do, my little rulebreaker."

"I'll show you everything I've brought first." He unzips the bag. "You can veto anything you aren't interested in, and I'll make a note of it." He turns to look at me over his shoulder, and it's only then that I realize I've tiptoed up behind him to get a better look.

His gaze is assessing, so much so that I take a hesitant step backward.

"Where did I leave you?" he questions in a murmur, gentle, yet cautioning.

Slowly I lower myself back down, one knee at a time. His piercing gaze ignites something between us. "That's my good girl," he comments with a smirk. Turning his attention back to the unzipped duffle bag he tells me, "I'm looking forward to playing with you tonight."

The first item he hands me is a soft leather blindfold in deep burgundy. It's simple with matching silk ties, but feels luxurious. It's certainly not cheap. His compliment brings a warmth to my chest when he says, "The color suits you."

"Thank you."

Taking it back from me, he sets it gently on the corner of the bed. It's unmade and it's the first time I've even considered making the bed since I've been home. Before my thoughts are allowed to wander, he tells me, "You respond well to praise. It's kept me from degrading you." I don't miss how he gauges my reaction.

"Degradation, like calling me a whore, spitting, and all that?" I question, not sure how it makes me feel anymore. It's been a long time since before James.

"What do you think of all of that?"

I take a moment to consider it. Even in my wildest days, it was mild and I was too intoxicated or well past any limit where I would object. Every touch heightened the high. It was different then.

I've been called a lot of things, like "little slut" and "my whore." I remember a time when I loved degradation, it was a part of the scene. It's a kink that I never imagined would leave me. If a man used it outside of the bedroom, it was obviously different. But within the confines of four walls, it's different because I know I'm going to get mine and when it's all said and done, they'd kiss me and tell me what a good girl I was. That was so long ago, though. A lifetime ago. "At one point I enjoyed it."

"But now?"

"I really just want to please you."

A huff of humor leaves Zander and he says, "Well that makes two of us." He doesn't waste any time pulling out the second item.

"Matching tape."

"Tape?" The hitch in my voice gives away my hesitancy as Zander holds out a roll of shiny tape in the same deep burgundy shade as the blindfold.

"It only sticks to itself," he explains, pulling the end free and holding it out for me to feel.

"It's like PVC tape?"

He nods in response to my question.

"Any objections?" he asks and his tone is neutral. "I know you want to please me, but you should know it would piss me off if you didn't object if you wanted to."

Shock at his darkened tone drops my bottom lip slightly. My eyes widen and he stares down at me with a seriousness. Kneeling in front of me, he drops the roll into my hand, lowers his lips to my ear and whispers, his warm breath trailing down the curve of my neck, "I want to feel you come on my dick as many times as you possibly can before you safe word." My breathing quickens as he leans back, brushing the hair from my face with a casualness that downplays the perversion he just spoke. "It'll make it harder for me if you lie right now."

"I was nervous because it's tape, but it won't stick to me, like duct tape would."

"Not at all."

Gripping the tape tighter, I ask him, "How do you plan to use it?"

"I'll bind your legs, so they're bent and you're easier to position however I want, and your hands and arms ... I haven't decided yet." His words drift off and his eyes roam down my body before he looks back up at me. "Or maybe some other binding. Do you have a preference?"

"No."

"Then however the hell I want. I may tie you to the bed frame. Strap you down so you can't move an inch while I fuck you ..." Leaving me with the vision of my wrists being cuffed to the bedposts with this tape, Z turns his back to me, fishing for something in the duffle before pulling out a pair of small silver safety scissors.

Nodding, I hand him back the heavy roll, his fingers brushing against mine and eliciting a rush of adrenaline and heat. "Then no objections."

A shiver runs down my back with my hair tickling along my shoulders. Every little touch feels heightened knowing I'll be bound and blindfolded.

The apprehension is an aphrodisiac.

"What should I call you?"

Zander's brow arches. "Like when we're in here ... when we're ..." A long exhale leaves me, my chest rising and falling with the newly found heat.

"You call me Z," he answers easily. Although I'm well aware he's toying with me.

"That's just a nickname."

"Like 'my little jailbird,'" he comments affectionately. He wears a simple smile yet somehow, there's pride hidden within it.

"I really—" I start to say love. I was going to say love it when he calls me that. Little bird was cute. Jailbird, though ... I love it when he calls me that. Swallowing down my admission, I clarify, "I mean, should I call you Sir when we're in a scene ... or something else?"

James like it when I called him Sir. And I loved it. I loved being in a room with him, knowing he could do whatever he wanted and that by the end of the night we'd both be sated and even more in love with each other than we were the day before.

"Two things. The first is that we will always be in scene. There isn't a moment where I will hesitate to reward or punish you. Is that understood?"

"Yes." The word rushes out of me with more want than I previously knew existed.

"Second. I've barely touched you, Ella. I only just tasted you last night. Honorifics like Master and Sir are earned. It means something more than ... the name of an avatar in a game. It's like a collar."

"How do you earn it?"

"A collar or an honorific?" he questions, the devilish look in his eye turning me on even more.

"We can consider it when you don't hesitate to tell me what's on your mind. When you trust that if I'm asking you a question, it's because I want nothing but the truth. That my opinion of you and our relationship will remain as it is regardless of what you tell me. That I'll protect you from all things, including all that insecurity, all that fear, everything and anything that could keep you from being content."

All I can do is whisper, "So serious." His thumb graces my lower lip, trailing along it until I part my lips as Zander slips the tip of his thumb into my mouth. His pointer curls under my chin and he tilts my head up, staring deep into my eyes.

"That mouth of yours is going to get you in trouble," he warns. Then he informs me, "We're only getting started, Ella. I have yet to break you in and toy with you." A wicked grin plays along his handsome face. My heart pounds harder as he drops his grip and brushes the hair from my face. "You have no idea how much I'm looking forward to breaking you in."

Heat rushes to my cheeks, but even more heat pools in my core. Longing for him to touch me there. No, needing him there.

My desperation urges a soft sound from my lips. It's not quite a moan, and merely an audible exhale. Without breaking my gaze, Zander groans deep in his chest, "The fucking sounds you make..." With a gruff sound he turns away from me, tossing the duffle bag with more force than necessary to the floor. It doesn't escape me that there is more in it, but I'm not given a moment to question what it could be.

Instead, Z commands me, "Get on the bed, I'm ready to play with you."

CHAPTER 10

ZANDER

Ready to play is an understatement. I'm rock hard, my adrenaline pounding, ready. Ella is so fucking beautiful with her cheeks flushed like that. So willing. So submissive. I want her under more of my control. I want all of her.

We'll take it slow so she learns what she's agreed to. It hasn't escaped me that she compares what she had before to what we're doing now, and there's no chance in hell that James knew what the fuck he was doing. They toyed around with the idea of submission. I have every intention of training her to *be* my submissive.

It's essential that I don't dive in too deep with her too fast, though I want to. God, I want to. Every inch of me craves every inch of her with a physical longing.

Four-count breaths. Four of them. Trailing along the edge of each of the additional toys I bought just for her, I control everything. I have to be in control of myself before I can be in control of her. I have to stay in control of myself, damn it.

She perches on her knees on the edge of the bed, her nightgown a silk puddle next to her. I approach her slowly so she has time to take me in. To see how I rise above her. How much stronger. How much restraint I have. That's an easy one. Instead of pushing her back on the bed and abandoning myself to her, I run my fingers through her hair and arrange it over her bare shoulders. The shudder that runs down her teased skin travels lower and hardens her nipples. I'm careful with every touch, and Ella responds to it, her large dark eyes on mine. She trembles under my hand.

I could do this for fucking hours. It's a drug to me. To tease her and immediately receive this reaction. Her shuddered breaths and every small movement as she nervously waits on the bed for my next move are addictive.

Anticipation is an essential part of any scene. It's what adds the tension to the air and the color to her cheeks. With my voice low, it rumbles, giving away my desire that's barely contained. "What are you imagining right now, jailbird?"

"You," she says in a breathy voice. "With your hands on me. I don't—" Her face gets redder. "I don't know if I can give you specifics. So many things. Mostly just the—just the sensation of being—"

"Dominated?"

The air cracks with a heat between us, only inches separating each other. "Yes."

My muscles coil, holding back everything just so I can offer her my thumb running down her bottom lip. Taking one step back, putting space between us, but keeping her gaze locked in mine, I tell her, "You're going to be good for me."

I phrase it as a statement and not a question to fill her with confidence. She can do this, and I believe in her. I know how she needs this.

Ella nods, a sheen coming to her eyes. "Yes," she whispers. "Yes. I am."

It's another reminder that I have to be gentle and guide her into this lifestyle. She thinks she knows what she's getting, but she doesn't have a fucking clue.

"I'm going to blindfold you now. Hands in your lap."

My little jailbird closes her eyes before the burgundy leather even touches her. She's so fucking good for me.

I fasten it over her eyes, testing to make sure it's snug. Ella's nipples peak and I allow myself an opportunity to run my knuckles down her skin, until they run over those hardened nubs. The small moan from her parted lips and the way she attempts to prevent her back from arching are everything I've wanted since I first saw her.

"How does it feel?" I murmur.

Her tongue flicks out to wet her lips. "It feels like

everything's been heightened. The air on my skin. The sound of your voice. It makes me question—" She stops herself, shaking her head.

"What does it make you question?"

"That's not the right word for it. It makes me think that I trust you. It wouldn't feel good to have my sight taken away like this if I didn't trust you. And I feel—I feel safe." More color floods to her cheeks. "Nervous, but safe."

"Good." I'm deliberately loud as I pick up the roll of tape from the bed and let her hear me unspool a length of it. She shudders at the sound. "Because I'm going to bind you now."

If I were selfish, I wouldn't bother to bind her. The sight of her as she is, sprawled out and waiting, her pale skin flushed, her lips parted and her chest rising and falling with anticipation is intoxicating.

She would fight the urge and I'd love to see her try and fail. To punish her for not being in control of her body for me. A low groan of want leaves me and I disguise it with a comment.

"Turn onto your belly, legs spread wide and hands behind your back."

There are plenty of toys I could have used instead of tape. Bondage gear and straps. The tape allows me to take my time and it's far less frightening for a submissive who hasn't been bound before.

Her breathing quickens as I draw out the tape, giving her the simple command to lift her chest off the bed. I let her feel it glide against her skin so she can feel for herself that it's not going to hurt her.

It doesn't require much tape at all to bind her, but the sound, the sensation, the prolonged time will make it appear far more than it is. I don't let her know that. I let her sit in the feeling of being helpless at my hands.

I go so slow my cock twitches. Whenever I grab her small body, maneuvering her as I need, she lets out the most innocent gasps. With my erection pressed into her thigh, I lean down and whisper at the shell of her ear, "You're doing so well." With a small peck on her shoulder, I add, "Good girl."

My sweet girl smiles, even through her shaky breath. "Thank you," she whispers, her lips trying to find mine. I could leave her there, not allowing her to seek out a damn thing while we're in this scene. But then I'd be denying myself, and I'm man enough to admit I want to kiss her as badly as she wants to kiss me. She's eager when my lips meet hers, her body arching, although her arms have already begun to be bound.

Tsking, I pull away. "Be my good girl."

Nodding eagerly, she moans that she will as I gently place her back down where I want her, my hand splaying against her shoulder blade, keeping her there so I can continue.

The tape groans as I pull more of it, and every time I do, her body shudders with her instinct to move.

She hasn't set any boundaries when it comes to being

bound, but sometimes subs don't know what those are until you're in the moment. Ella's lips part, her body coming alive with more tension, but she doesn't protest. Doesn't use her safe word.

Ella's breathing is heavier and her entire chest is flushed by the time I run my fingertips down her inner thighs after binding her thighs to her calves. The small moans she gives me are fucking everything. She can't close her legs to me, but she tries. On instinct. I know she doesn't want to; controlling a natural reaction is difficult and something tells me Ella doesn't have a damn bit of experience when it comes to that. As I move off the bed to observe her, I give the command, "Don't move," and the words are nearly caught in the back of my throat when I see how fucking wet she is for me. Her seam glistens with arousal.

It takes her a moment to relax into her bindings. As the sheets rustle beneath her, all I do is wait. It's obvious that she's trying so hard to stay still, but not hard enough. She'll learn the way to stay completely still is to submit to it the way she should be submitting to me, with everything she has. Ella's not there yet. I haven't had enough time with her. But I will. My blood heats at the thought of spending hours on this. Days and days of praising her while she gets off on obeying.

Speaking of obedience—

With a hand on each of her thighs, I flip her over. Without any warning, she yelps, the sound high and feminine and all Ella. A rough chuckle leaves me as she lies on the bed naked, legs spread and completely bared to me. Even as she catches her breath I know she can hear my pleasure in the low groan from the sight of her. Hearing and touch are her most prominent senses right now, which means everything I do in those realms carries more weight.

"You're at my mercy now, jailbird," I whisper and then easily flip her again so her arms aren't behind her, uncomfortably supporting her weight. "Do you remember your safe word?" The question is as much of a reminder for her as it is a way for me to ensure she's still in the right frame of mind. Deprivation can play tricks on even the most mentally sound. For a grieving widow … well, I haven't forgotten her struggles.

"Yes," Ella whispers back.

"Good girl."

The first vibrator is ready for me. Ella turns her head so her other cheek is against the comforter, her shoulders rising and falling with every breath she takes. I flip the switch and the vibrations fill the air. I let it go on long enough that it takes over. What else can she hear, other than this? Nothing. I make sure the sound of the vibrator is everything. She waits, patient and submissive. Not that she has any other choice. Ella's helplessly bound, her hands behind her back, her legs spread open for me, and—

When I'm done with her, I'll climb onto the bed behind her

and drive myself into her slick wetness until we're both spent. The desire to do that right fucking now is overwhelming. I need her as much as she needs me. Four-count breaths. In and out, focusing on control. On conditioning her to listen and trust, to obey above everything else. Even when the tempting release of pleasure is so very close.

"You will obey me, my little jailbird. I have a set of rules and there will be consequences if you don't abide by them. You need to do as you're told. Do you understand?"

Ella nods behind her blindfold. Her hands open and close again.

Just as my hand raises to swat her ass for not verbalizing her answer, she murmurs, "Yes, I will obey."

With my pulse rising, the adrenaline fueling each of my thoughts, I ask, "Was it like that between you and James?"

Tension runs through her like an electric shock. Ella goes completely still, her breath stopped and her thighs rigid and unmoving. I keep my eyes on her body, every curve down to the detail of how tight the cords in her neck are. Checking every muscle. Monitoring what I can see of her expression.

Did I push her past some hidden boundary? *The mention of his name.* It's hell to wait without touching her, but I do it. This is something that can't be rushed. I'm going to do what any good Dom would do, and what I know to be right.

"Would you rather I refer to him as your former Dom?"

Ella bites her bottom lip. "Either is fine," she whispers

and then clears her throat. "And ... no. He didn't have a list for me." There's obvious confusion in her tone.

"There is no one way to be submissive and no correct way to be a Dominant. But you will find I have my desires, and that includes control and obedience. Is that understood?"

"Yes." The second the word is uttered from her lips, I press the vibrator to her clit, letting it sit there as she screams out.

With her hands restrained behind her, her legs bound and spread, I use my other hand to press her chest into the bed. Although she cries out in sudden pleasure, the only movements are the curling of her toes and her head thrashing from side to side. Her body is tense and I know that only intensifies the pleasure radiating through her.

"Be still, and take it like a good girl," I command her and she does as she's told, biting down on her lip. As her strangled cry leaves her, her body bucks and bows with her release.

I can barely make out the apology on her lips and I ignore it.

"Did you come?"

Her body shudders and she's quick to nod and then correct herself, staying still as she answers yes hesitantly.

"You are not allowed to come again, not until I tell you that you can. Understood?"

Her answer is delayed, and I imagine she doubts she has the ability to obey. "Yes," she finally says and then swallows thickly, her body finally relaxing.

I hover the vibrator closer to her shoulder, taking my

time. Closer and closer and closer until it grazes her nipple that's pressed against the sheet. Ella gasps, trying to resist arching away, but she can't. I've bound her too skillfully to leave her room to wriggle over the bed. "I'm going to make you a list of tasks to complete every day."

This point is easily emphasized by circling her nipples with the vibrator again. I play with the other one, testing its weight in my hand and listening to those sweet moans.

Fuck, I need her now. I can barely think with the sight of her helpless beneath me.

"We'll go over the list tomorrow."

Placing the vibrator beneath her, I let it rest against her clit as I unzip my pants and then drop them to the floor. Her moans turn to breathy whimpers as I climb onto the bed behind her. The bed dips from my weight and Ella strains against the tape. Staring between her thighs I watch as her pussy clenches around nothing, slowly removing the vibrator and turning it off. She gasps the moment it's taken away, as if she's been holding her breath. God, she wants this. And I want it to be so much sensation for her that she has to give herself up to me. She needs to submit more than she already has. She needs to learn to do it, damn it, because that's the only way I know to keep her present. It's the only way I know to heal her.

I notch myself to her slick, hot entrance and thrust home in one stroke.

Hard. Possessive. Like she's mine.

She is mine, and her clit is mine too. I reach the vibrator around her and press it directly to that bundle of nerves again, although I'm more than aware it must be overly sensitive now. Ella cries out. This is intense for her, and I know for certain because her body has made it intense for me. Her muscles squeeze me, going tight and tighter. She can't actually change her position. The tape keeps her in place.

She has a safe word and she knows it.

Ella has never been more beautiful than she is with all her weight pressed against her bindings. It's a fucking gorgeous struggle. Her muscles tense as she tries to stay still for me because I ordered her to do it, but she can't let go. The vibrator is driving her to a new, expansive pleasure as her walls tighten around my cock, forcing a tingling need up my spine.

"Wait," I tell her through gritted teeth. "Wait, jailbird. You don't come until I tell you to."

"No," Ella says in a breathy voice, and quickly adds in desperation, "Please." I won't punish her now because she doesn't even know she's said it. It's pure begging, pure pleading, and I don't give in.

I angle the vibrator more firmly over her clit. "Good girls come when they're told to come." She clenches around me at the praise. She loves it. She can't get enough of being told what a good fucking girl she is. New arousal coats my cock as I lean down to whisper in the curve of her neck, letting my warm breath trail there, "Good girl. My perfect jailbird. It's so hard not to come, and you're doing so well."

A shiver runs down her back and her pleas turn to whimpers that she buries in the sheets.

I brace one hand on the bed and fuck her with deep, long strokes. All the way in. All the way out. Every thrust presses against her inner walls, with no more room to spare. Stretching her. I don't want this to be over yet. I don't want to be finished with this pleasure. It's mine too. It starts in the base of my cock and spreads outward along every inch of me. Up my spine. Down my legs to my toes. Every muscle works together to fuck her harder, but not faster. I've never concentrated harder than keeping this vibrator on her clit. Practice in obedience for her. Practice in domination for me.

It makes me feel almost drunk, this power. A few words is all it takes to get her to stop an orgasm for me. Ella's mouth opens, trying to get air to cry. She's close.

"Please, Z," she begs. "I'm trying to be good."

"You need to come?"

I'm being harsh, and I know it. Pleasure is just as intense as pain. They're two sides of the same coin. "Yes," Ella answers, her voice rising. "I need to come."

"Please," she cries out again when I don't answer. Her head thrashes once, barely tugging the blindfold up.

"I can't stop it and I don't—" She bites down on the sheets and I fuck her slower, moving the vibrator up just slightly.

Her breathing is heavier. It gives her a moment for her orgasm to lessen slightly. I barely hear her beg me again and then reason, "I don't want you to be unhappy with me."

God. Such a perfect submissive. She tries and tries and tries. I couldn't have asked for better.

I remove the vibrator, and instantly Ella collapses away from me as much as possible. She can't move much. The tape is too strong, but she tries. I give her three long seconds of trying to live without the vibrator and push it against her clit again while thrusting into her harder and faster.

"Come for me, jailbird," I say into her ear, and she explodes around my cock, gripping me as she shudders and shakes. It's a cascade of pleasure and heat and it almost makes me come.

But I'm not done fucking her.

I drop the vibrator, turn her over, and drive my hips between her spread legs. I'm conscious of her hands behind her back, and her arms, and I keep it in mind while I fuck her with primal need. Her body is so pretty, arched for me this way. Her neck is exposed. Her breasts. I take one of her nipples and roll it between my finger and thumb. Over and over and over. It's not a particularly unforgiving movement, not really, but if I do it enough, she'll—

"Oh." The sound stretches out and out and out. "Oh," she says again.

Her voice almost pushes me over the edge, but I pull away and flip her over again. I want to be inside her heat. It seems like the only thing keeping me on earth. Her hot, wet pussy trying to get me further inside.

I circle her asshole with a fingertip. She's helpless to stop me, and Ella shivers when I do it. "Have you been taken here?"

"No," she whispers.

I work a finger into her pussy beside my cock. And then I bring it back to that tight little hole. Ella groans when I push my fingertip in, lubricated with her arousal, and gasps when I give her the rest.

And then I grab the vibrator.

One touch to her clit and she's off, crying out, crying hard. Coming yet again. Her pants fuel me to keep playing, toying with her, pushing her boundaries slowly yet steadily.

I pull myself free from her as she comes down. Giving her a moment, I take out the scissors after cleaning off my hands with a wet wipe.

"Stay still." The safety scissors easily cut through the bindings within seconds, releasing her body to fall onto the bed.

She's still unsteady from the aftershocks so I have to prop her up with my hands to get her on her knees. "Take off the blindfold."

Ella pulls it down with shaking hands, leaving it around her neck.

"Hands and knees, jailbird. I want you to watch the mirror now."

She gets to her hands and knees, still trembling, her dark eyes locked on me in the mirror as I climb behind her, line myself up, and take her again. She's a gorgeous sight. Her hair a messy halo, her cheeks flushed. Every thrust shakes her. Her breasts sway with the motion of my hips. I fuck her like I've wanted to since she first talked to me, hard and unforgivingly, until I'm close to the edge of my own pleasure. Seconds away.

I need to see her face. I turn Ella and position her on my lap as I fall to the bed. Her small hands land on my chest to steady herself. My hips thrust up and she's far too weak to keep herself upright. She drapes her arms over my shoulders and holds on for dear life.

And she kisses me.

Her lips capture mine with a need that's unexpected.

What that single kiss does to me is a shock I hadn't anticipated. It strikes me how obvious it is that she was desperate for it. She tastes both sweet and sinful.

"Fuck," I grunt into the crook of her neck as my orgasm tears out of me.

She holds me just as tightly as I hold her as she finds her release with mine.

As she's lying lifeless on top of me, I kiss the crown of her head and whisper without thinking twice about it, "You don't know what you do to me."

CHAPTER 11

ELLA

"A wash and wave?" Kam comments. "And I like the all white," he adds before I can respond. His four fingers do a half wave as he gestures toward my hands.

"The manicurist suggested it." I peek down at my nails as the waiter arrives with a tall skinny glass of unsweetened tea. "Thank you," I manage to get out in time for him to give a smile and nod.

The Fooleries has been remodeled since we were last here. Seated on the outside balcony, there's a heat lamp already blazing in each of the corners. The balcony only has three small circular iron tables, fitted with a robin's-egg-blue tablecloth. Everything else is white. The menus, napkins and single candle burning in the center of each table.

"You really like the white?" I question before popping one of the almonds from a small bowl of mixed nuts that was on the table into my mouth. Kam loves the walnuts, so I leave all of those pieces for him.

"Very in. Very chic ... Angels and virgins wear white, but I've always thought it looks just as good on the sinful."

Kam's comment gets a laugh from me. "I wasn't sure at first," I say and shrug, lifting the glass up, "but I like it." The last bit comes out raspy and my fingers press against my throat before I sip the cold beverage.

When I set the glass down and peer back at Kam, his expression is riddled with concern. "How are you feeling?"

An anxiousness sweeps through my body at the realization that the pain I felt was a reminder of what Zander did to me last night. More specifically, my cries and moans for him to fuck me harder, but for Kam, it's a reminder of something entirely different.

"Fine," I answer easily, reaching for the cloth napkin and laying it across my lap.

"Well, you look beautiful. You look—" His words falter and I'm not sure what he planned to say, but what comes out after an exhale is only a reiteration of his first statement. "Just beautiful."

"It was Zander's suggestion," I confide in him in an attempt to usher the conversation away from wherever Kam's carefully navigating. I know my throat, my voice even, has to be a reminder of what I did while at the center. "He said I should get my hair and nails done today. This morning he handed me a credit card, then told me he made appointments and that Silas would be driving me, so I should get my ass ready to go and be pampered." I add for good measure, "And if I wasn't ready on time, he'd spank me."

Kam's movements stop midway as he was picking up his napkin and the silverware clangs on the table. I can't help but laugh.

"Well I'm glad one of us is smiling," he chides.

"Oh please," I admonish him in return, a genuine smile pulling up my spirits. "Since when did you become such a prude?"

Humor lights his eyes. He even smiles as he rearranges the cutlery and places the napkin across his lap as I have. "He's controlling."

"Like James was," I reply without considering what I was saying until the comparison left me. Another wave of that anxiousness comes over me, but it quickly vanishes.

"And I told you to dump his ass too." There's a fondness, a nostalgia in Kam's comment.

"I remember that," I say and my smile falters only slightly. The rawness in my throat comes back but this time it carries a prick to the back of my eyes as well.

"I mean, obviously I was wrong about that one," Kam says offhandedly and I realize we're speaking about him. Talking about James in the past tense. I don't have long to dwell on the thought. "He went from a *good time*," Kam adds, lowering his voice at the insinuation, "to taking all your time."

I can't help but smile, even if there's a painful longing in my chest. "He took his time, though." I roll my eyes at the thought and resort to picking up my iced tea once again. It's tart, making my lips pucker after a sip before I reach for the sugar.

"What was it? It took him what, a year?" he asks me, and it's easy. It turns easy, thinking about how we came to fall in love. How he went from a man I wanted and enjoyed the occasional fling with, to a man who only wanted me and who I couldn't imagine living my life without.

"Every third Saturday for …" I trail off, peeking up past the heat lamp and spot a small blue jay on the roof. "Maybe four months it was just that one night?"

"At Monet's, right?" I nod in response, the memories filtering back to me. It was a good time. That's all *he* was. We ran in the same circles. Knew the same people. One night, after I'd been avoiding him, teasing him, leading him on … we hit it off and had a romp in the sheets. It was a fling, a damn good fling. I thought it would only be that one night, but the next month, at the same gathering, he made it known in no uncertain terms that I'd be with him again that night.

"And then it was house calls and almost nine months later is when he got in that fight with Taylor."

Kam's brow raises and he lifts his coffee mug and then

says, "Oh yes, and that would be the moment I told you to dump his ass."

Biting down on my lip I remember that entire ordeal as Kam continues, "He couldn't call you his girlfriend, but he could start some shit with Taylor." Taylor's no one really. He's the son of a hotshot, who's hot as fuck himself. He got through life on good looks. He's nice enough, but he wasn't looking for anything more than a good time. Which was fine, 'cause that's what I was after too. I figured James only wanted me the once, or else he would have called. He would have reached out. So I made my move for Taylor and that's when James intervened.

With a one-shoulder shrug I remind him, "I might have been the one to start it ... technically."

Kam's laugh is as genuine as it is enthusiastic. "That's right," he says and his smile is contagious. "Now I remember that reporter with the press article that we had to pay off."

I hum at the memory. "The truth was much better than fiction." As the waiter brings the avocado caprese salad, which looks divine drizzled with a thick balsamic vinegar, I lean back in the chair to give him room.

"The truth always is better than fiction," Kam comments and then smiles up at the waiter to thank him. I don't miss how the waiter gives Kam a longer glance than he gave me.

Speaking of hot men, I think as I watch the tall young man, he's got to be no older than midtwenties. In other words, way too young for Kam. And it's quite obvious he's interested in Kam.

"Flirt," I speak beneath my breath and smirk at Kam the moment the waiter has left us.

Kam has the audacity to deny it as the blush reaches his cheeks. He's freshly shaven so it can't hide behind stubble.

My fork spears through the ripe tomatoes and I let Kam pretend that I've forgotten. The bird I saw a moment ago flutters in a way that steals my gaze. He's a vibrant blue, perched on the edge and more than likely waiting for scraps.

"So," Kam gets my attention before asking, "is Zander your boyfriend then?" He raises a single brow in question.

With a thump in my chest, I don't know how to answer him so I retreat to draining the rest of my tea. Twirling the straw forces the ice to clink against the glass. After an awkward moment, I ask him, "I thought we were going to discuss selling my properties ... and you know? Moving on." I hate the term. I'll never move on. Damon says you move through it, and there's a piece that's always there. I prefer that.

His expression drops as he nods, his tone more serious. "It's not the best time to sell, so we could wait, and sell when the market's better. Or if you'd rather just be done with it, we'll still get a good deal, just maybe not a great one. Either way, whatever you feel comfortable with, we can maneuver."

Whatever I feel comfortable with. His words repeat in my head as the memories filter back. I can't stop them. Just thinking of our home together, of the furniture, the majority of it his, I can barely keep myself composed when I remember how we broke in the dark gray Old English-style sofa of our first place together. So many firsts happened in that house.

"Let's sell them." I push the words out. "The main home and the two vacation properties down south."

"And the belongings?" Kam's question is gentle and I nod in response, picking up my drink to find it empty. I shake the glass, rattling the ice and with the straw I drain the tiniest bit of tea until there's nothing left.

"And what about where you're currently staying?" he asks cautiously. "The lodge?"

"We can keep it," I answer him. "We were barely there together." Fuck. It's not like ripping off a Band-Aid at all. Not when the wound is still raw and bleeding.

"And the west wing?"

His answering question hangs in the air between us.

"What of it?" I say in a whisper. I don't want it mentioned.

"We still have it closed off ..."

When all I have is silence, he offers, "Maybe we redecorate it?"

I focus on pushing around the remainder of the food on my plate. Staring at the crumbs and remembering how that's what hurt the most. Laying in a bed we shared, and waking up alone.

"Did Zander suggest anything else?"

"What?"

He gestures toward me, his tone relaxed and casual. As if he could disguise the fact that he's attempting to change the subject since the current one has turned heavy. "Hair and nails. Does he want you to go to the spa too? Maybe to a lingerie boutique?"

Although his tone is humorous, my response is flat. "He wants me to create a new normal that would make me happy." I force a smile, remembering how we went through the checklist two days ago. He sat with me while I made the necessary arrangements and Silas accompanied me to them, acting more as a chauffeur than anything else.

"A new normal?" Kam's back straightens, his reaction not at all contained.

"We made a list," I say after taking a deep breath in and leaning back in the chair. My appetite has vanished.

"A list of what you want your normalcy to be?" Kam questions and I nod. He nods along with me. "So what else is there, other than nails and hair?"

Chewing the inside of my cheek, I keep myself from reaching into my purse to take out the list and instead tell Kam only the ones he needs to know.

"Things like, make my bed in the morning and practice yoga before noon like I used to." I'm quick to add, "I have daily affirmations."

"What affirmations?" Kam asks, and judging by his

expression, I know he's still wary of Zander. I get it. I do.

"I will allow myself to feel grief and then let it go," I tell him after inhaling slowly and Kam's eyes widen slightly. "Damon approved it."

Kam nods as he looks away, obviously uncomfortable but he says, "There was an affirmation I was using a bit ago."

"Really?"

He meets my gaze to tell me, "When Gerald broke up with me." His expression sobers. They were engaged and I still don't know what happened; all I know is that I wasn't around when they broke up. I was at the center.

Sucking in a breath, he tells me, "I give myself permission to do what is right for me." He swallows thickly.

"I like that one. I really do."

He pouts at my smile, a goofy expression on his face. "You should add that to your list."

"I think I will."

"Yoga, affirmations, anything else he wants in your new normal?" He returns to picking away at his chicken caesar wrap.

Shaking my head, I don't tell him the hair and nails, and even my chosen outfit for the day, is all Zander's choosing. My grooming and appearance are to please him. It's a requirement for every day.

Along with accepting a list every day of what I should accomplish while he's gone. He's busy arranging everything in his new place nearby. I haven't seen it yet, but he said once he has everything in order, since things have gotten chaotic with his leave from The Firm, then I can come see and maybe stay if Cade will allow it.

Kam asks in a humorous tone, "What about daily blow jobs?"

His last question is spoken at the same moment the waiter returns to refill my tea. I can't help the grin that slips across my face at the sight of Kam's embarrassment.

The waiter remains professional, although he's obviously heard and has a hard time keeping a smile from creeping onto his face that would match mine. "Anything else I can get you?"

Kam asks for the check and I'm grateful he seems to forget about the list after the young man leaves.

"Speaking of blow jobs," I murmur and prod him. "Anything new in your dating world?"

My playfulness falls flat. Kam's lips are pressed in a thin line. "Gerald wants to get back together. He called a couple of nights ago and again last night."

I'm surprised by how happy his admission makes me. "You two were so good together."

Again the optimism does nothing but faceplant on the table.

"When you were away ... he didn't do things he should have. Not like I needed him to."

My throat dries and once again, I'm left with an anxiousness that comes with those memories.

"Enough of that," he says matter-of-factly. "To a new

normal," Kam offers in cheers, his tone a little more upbeat. It only takes me a moment to force a smile and my glass of water, since the tea is empty, meets his.

"To a new normal."

And so that's how time passes, checking off a list daily, letting Zander fuck me into contentedness and pretending this new normal feels right and not like I'm counting the days until something inevitably goes wrong, very, very wrong and entirely out of my control.

CHAPTER 12

ZANDER

It feels like several lifetimes have passed since I let Quincy walk away from me into the night. Time seemed to drag on forever after she was murdered. Guilt is a heavy, relentless emotion. It makes the body move slower and time crawl, except during the moments when you think it might be lifting. It always comes back, though. The guilt is never resolved. No amount of therapy has been able to free me from it. I'll live with that guilt until I die.

If I had stopped her and done what I wanted to do, done what I know she needed, she'd be here. She'd be alive and happy. Probably with someone else, but she'd breathing.

I know all the things to think, and all the things to say. I know how to organize my thoughts from the physical world around me to the emotional world inside my mind. I've practiced holding these things at arm's length and observing them without sinking into them. But no matter how many times I logic my way around Quincy's death, I still end up at the same conclusion.

I bear some responsibility. It's not all my fault, of course, though it felt like it at the time. The man who murdered Quincy bears more of that burden. He's the one who mugged her and then killed her. He took her life.

I can't describe the hate I have for him to senselessly take her life.

I'm still not ready for the hearing.

It takes a disgusting amount of time for these cases to work their way through the courts. She's been gone two years and we're just now reaching the point where the case is before the judge.

Ella and I move gingerly around each other in her house before it's time to leave. The guilt feels so heavy on days like this. No reasoning my way out of it this time. I have to sit with it, and sit in the knowledge that something new will happen today with Quincy's case, regardless of whether justice is served or not.

"Are you nervous?" Ella asks me in the car on the way over. I don't miss how her black heels slip against one another nervously. I haven't told her much. Only that Quincy was a good friend turned lover and a former submissive, and that she was murdered. Her only comment was whispered, *so you're mourning too*, which I didn't respond to.

"About the outcome of the case?"

"Yeah."

"No."

She watches me with those beautiful dark eyes, her expression open. "Do you think it's already decided, then?" She's gentle with her questioning, which is different for her. It's a careful tone, like she's afraid that it'll hurt me.

It warms something inside of me, knowing she cares. She is good. All things good in this world. My hand lays on top of hers, my fingers slipping between hers to hold her hand loosely.

"There's more than enough evidence. The DA told someone I know that he's hoping for a lesser sentence if it looks like he'll get off. He wants to plea it down." I keep my eyes on the road and my breathing steady. "No amount of prison time will bring her back. But this is how she gets her day. Other people will be—" I cut myself off with a deep breath and I pull my hand away to pull onto the highway. "Other people will hear about her today, what happened to her, and that seems right. That her death will be acknowledged." My throat's tighter than I'd like and the car is warmer than it should be. "It's a two-hour drive," I tell her, "so get comfortable, little bird."

I turn down the heat and we drive mostly in silence.

She holds my hand, though. Every chance she gets. Hers is small in mine, but her grip tells me she's not going to let go unless I want her to.

When we get to the front of the courthouse and I let go to take her tweed coat, her cheeks are still flushed from the chill of the short walk in here.

It's nearly ten degrees colder here. I fucking hate the cold.

I'm picking up my phone from the bin at the courthouse metal detectors when the text comes in.

Cade: You doing okay?

It's the first real communication we've had since the coffee shop and my immediate instinct is to ignore him. He knows that I don't want to talk about it. It also pisses me off that he hasn't asked about Ella. Not once. Although it's possible he's been keeping tabs on everything through Damon. More than likely actually. The last thought softens my resolve.

With Ella's heels clicking on the marble tile, we take our seats near the back of the courtroom and Ella scoots close to my side while I answer Cade. When she reaches for my right hand to hold, and sees the phone, she politely withdraws, but I make a point to move my phone to the left and take her hand in mine. I can feel her gaze on the side of my face, but I don't say anything. All I do is run my thumb over her knuckles as I text my brother back with one hand.

Zander: I'm doing all right.

Cade: I know Ella came with you for the hearing.

Cade: I think it's a good thing.

The defensiveness that spiked at his first message is

quickly dissolved by the second. It's unexpected for him to approve anything at all that has to do with Ella. It's a relief that he's being agreeable about this. It's like one brick in the wall between us is showing cracks.

Zander: I do too. I'm glad she's here.

Cade: How is she?

Zander: Quiet, yet full of questions. My response makes me smile and I glance over at Ella, this beautiful woman by my side who's taking in the courtroom and watching each of the people who file in. I recognize a handful of them, Quincy's friends and family who offer me nods, quiet hellos and a squeeze of my shoulder from Quincy's father.

I don't say much and neither do they. They all notice Ella, though, and their hesitant smiles offer me only a modicum of comfort.

She wears a simple black sheath dress that still manages to look expensive, her hair in a twist behind her head, and she looks exactly as prim and proper as the day I first saw her. Exactly as elegant. Some things are different, of course— there's a light in her eyes now that wasn't there before. She's not so silent. But anyone looking at her now would never know what she'd been through. They'd see a gorgeous, delicate woman wearing a serious expression and sitting at my side. No more, no less.

There are many sides that people show. The broken man. The loyal brother. The confident Dom.

I'm not any of those today. Not completely. I've healed enough that I'm not going to lose my shit in the courtroom, but I can still feel the cracks in my heart that were left when that policeman showed up at my door.

I add, after a moment with him not responding, *She's good.*

Cade: Let me know how it goes and if you need anything.

The proceedings begin, and it's mostly a bunch of legal bullshit, the opening arguments and requests for changes to this or that. Which piece of evidence can be admitted. Who is representing whom. It all seems very clinical compared to the reality of the situation. No one mentions what the night air felt like on my face as she walked away from me. No one describes the reflection of the streetlights in her hair or the angry set of her shoulders. All of this is encapsulated with a few quick sentences. A statement from her then-partner Zander Thompson.

Of course I'm mentioned, but that amounts to nothing, just like my relationship with Quincy did. Other than her murderer, I was the last person to see her alive.

Ella stiffens at the mention of my name. I'm quick to move my arm around her, pulling her in and retaking her hand. She molds against me, warm and with a remorseful expression. My name is mentioned again, but those sentences are swallowed up by what happened after. I'm not on trial in this case, and neither is Quincy. It's her murderer who's on trial. A guy who's been rotting in a jail cell since his arrest two years ago. I feel no pity for him. Let him rot forever.

Was Quincy thinking about our conversation when she died? That's what I want to know. Before the murderer approached her, what was she going to do? Was she going to storm back over and scream at me for not wanting to get married? Was she going to apologize and tell me she loved me, even if I couldn't say it back?

No one mentions this, either. It's not part of a legal proceeding. Quincy becomes the body her assailant attacked. No mention of whether her face flushed with anger when he attacked her or went pale with fear. No mention of whether she screamed, or what she said. *Signs of a struggle. Lacerations on her temple and collarbone. Fifth metacarpal fracture.*

They can't see her, but I can. She took a swing at the guy. It wasn't enough.

My throat dries and I have to readjust, keeping back the emotions that threaten to overwhelm me. It's been two years, but there's no amount of time that could pass and make this right.

I take so many four-count breaths I lose track of them. Ella holds my hand tightly through the whole hearing. It's the longest we've touched each other. She refuses to let go and I'm grateful for her.

Quincy ended up in harm's way because she wanted more from me than the D/s relationship we had, and I didn't want that. I couldn't feel the spark for it, even though she was beautiful and smart. Something in my gut warned me away from that deeper commitment. And now I'm here with Ella, who also wants more than domination and submission. She wants it, even if she hasn't admitted it. Of course she wants it. She's been married before. She knows what it means to commit like that.

And with her—

My chest seems to expand with how much I want that too. The vision blocks out the court proceedings. If Ella were mine, she'd have my ring on her finger right now. I could feel it while she held my hand. It wouldn't be her home, but *our* home, somewhere else. It would be the two of us looking out at the world together. But then again ... would she ever want to move?

Peeking down at her, I know she was someone else's first. Someone she misses. Someone she hasn't let go of. I know it all too well.

There's also the logistics and legal blocks that would stand in our way. If Cade allows me to return to the company, there's no chance in hell I can be married to a former client. A current client. Trust is our main currency at The Firm. If potential applicants can't count on us to protect their lives and well-being, then we don't have a job. My brother's business will be destroyed. All kinds of suspicions would follow all of them everywhere.

The prosecution has brought out more evidence. Pictures, this time. Of the street where it happened, a yellow arrow pointing to where Quincy's body was found. Another photo. Another yellow arrow. This is where it happens.

Photos of Quincy.

The rush of blood fills my head, and Ella's grip on my hand tightens. I'm not going to lose control. I'm not going to sink into this firestorm of guilt and hate. I can witness it from a distance, the way I have to witness these photos. Rage slowly consumes me. *Breathe. Breathe.*

"Do you want to leave?" she murmurs into my ear. Both of her hands firmly around mine.

I offer her the single word although it comes out harsh and ragged. "No." I don't want to stay, but I'm not walking out now. I won't walk out now. I have to face this as much as Quincy's murderer does. I have to look at the consequences of my actions. Forcing myself to restrain every emotion, I tell her calmly, "We'll stay."

"Okay." Ella sounds even and sure. She's not disappointed that I want to stay, though I do glance over at her face in profile. Should I have brought her here? She's under the care of The Firm because her past caught up with her. Overwhelmed her.

"What about you?"

Ella's eyes come to mine, and I don't see an ounce of indecision there. "It's hard to look at," she says, keeping her voice low. "But I want to be with you for this."

I bring her hand to my lips and kiss her knuckles.

I'm so damn grateful she's here, and it brings back that overwhelming sense that she should be mine. In every way possible. Using the D/s relationship as the only framework for us seems like a cop-out, in a way. Saying that's all we can have is a lie. It's not true. There can be more. Another layer. If Ella wants it. If she really does want it, once all of this is over and she's not in The Firm's care. Not a minute before.

There's a brief recess where Ella insists I eat a granola bar, and then we're back in the courtroom for the defense to respond.

And that's when I see this is going to be different.

Murder cases like this often have trials that stretch out for days. Weeks, even. There's a shift in the energy in the room when we come back, the defense attorneys consulting in low voices at the front of the room. One of them approaches the bench, and the judge listens. Nods.

"What's happening?" asks Ella. "Can you hear?"

"No. But we'll know soon enough."

We do know soon enough. What happens is that the defense puts the murderer on the stands.

He's a tall guy, too thin and pale, with dark bags under his eyes. He's lost weight since they put his picture in the news for killing Quincy. I'd expected to feel pure fury when I saw him on the stand, but looking at him now, all I feel along with the rage is ...

Emptiness.

I've been staring at the back of his head all day, and seeing his face doesn't change anything. It doesn't change that Quincy is gone and never coming back. She'll be dead forever, and it will always have begun with our conversation.

Justice can be healing, though. We have to own our actions, but we cannot own anyone else's. This will change something. It will bring a sense of closure. There will be no more open case, no more phone calls, no more text messages. Quincy can rest and her name will be spoken by people who knew her beyond those photographs. The memories of her smiling will be the context of those conversations. And I'm ready for that. Fuck, I need that.

No more of this.

There's a brief back-and-forth between the murderer and the judge, and then the defendant, her murderer, a man named Elijah Edwards is holding a sheet of paper in his hands, staring down at it.

"Your Honor. Jury. Ladies and gentlemen in the courtroom." He sounds tired. "We're all here today because of what I did, and I won't sit in front of you and deny it. I killed Quincy Davis."

My next breath fails to come. A cold sweat breaks out along my skin as I sit still, barely contained and listen to him speak.

"I was high, on meth, when I encountered the young woman on the street that night. I don't say that to make an excuse, but to offer an explanation. I wasn't thinking straight, and I killed her. I—" He covers his mouth with his hand, then drops it down again. "I am truly, truly sorry for the pain I've caused to her friends and family, and I know that nothing I say here will ever make up for that. All I can tell you is that I live with the horror of what I've done every day. That I became a person who would take a life under the influence of drugs. It's not what I intended, and it's not the way I hoped my life would be. Your Honor, I understand that I don't deserve a second chance. All I ask is that you grant me mercy when you make your decision. I was in the grips of something I couldn't control." He puts the paper down. "That's all," he says. "That's all."

Chapter 13

Ella

I keep expecting him to cry. I did. Tears spilled helplessly once we were back in the car. If anything were to bring him to the brink, it would be the tombstones to the left of us.

"She's buried over there." He motions as we sit at the red light. His knuckles rap on the window although his focus is on the street.

"We could go, if you want?" I offer Zander, who shifts in his seat. Staring out of the window at the rows of headstones.

"No," he says and his answer is gentle, more composed than he's been. I learned today he's short when he's emotional. He's also quick to check on me once he realizes he's been blunt.

All I can do is to keep holding his hand.

I don't think souls stay in cemeteries. There's nothing

here but stone, dying flowers and grass that needs to be trimmed but with the chill in the air and fall turning colder in the mountains, it'll probably stay like this until spring.

"Are you all right?" he asks me yet again. The ache in my chest is the most vulnerable I've felt in so long and it's directly linked to the way he looks at me. And the question I keep wanting to ask him, but my heart refuses. *Did you love her?*

Instead I nod, saying that I'm all right, and question, "Did you come this way because you knew she was buried over there?"

"Yes ... Are you sure you're all right?"

"I'm fine. I haven't gone to where James is buried. I just don't think he's there. Have you been ... since she's been gone?"

"To the cemetery?" he questions, slowly hitting the gas and putting it in our rearview. "I used to. In the beginning."

I debate on whether or not to tell him something I haven't confided in anyone yet, but I settle on the truth, on speaking what's on my mind. I'll feel it, whatever the memory brings, and then let it go. "I would go to the bar a lot. When James first died."

"The bar?" he asks for clarification, and he peeks at me a moment before returning his attention to the road.

"There's this bar down by the trolley in the city we lived in; it's the first floor of Monet's. It's where we first met." I smile at the memory as the car moves and the world blurs around us in a beautiful hue of greens and blues. The trees are only just starting to turn to auburn shades. Licking my lower lip, I continue, staring out of the window. "I knew of him, of James," I say, correcting myself. "I knew he slept around. I'm sure he knew I did the same."

I can feel Zander's eyes on me, but I don't look back at him. Instead I remember the din of the bar and the way James smiled at me, like I would jump at the chance to fuck him. I'm certain I roll my eyes now just like I did back then. "He was cocky, came from money but invested in a few companies at the right time.

"Rich Prick is what we used to call him."

"Sounds like Prince Charming," Z jokes and I finally turn to him, letting him see how happy that comment made me. His strong hand lands on my thigh and I place mine on top of his, not wanting him to let go as I remember the first time I spoke to James, years ago.

"He wanted my number when I turned him down."

Z looks back at me, curious without an ounce of jealousy. His thumb travels over my hand as I tell him our story.

"He said he'd change my mind." My heart does a painful flip in my chest remembering the timbre of his voice. "There wasn't a chance in hell I was going to sleep with him. I was getting over a different guy. So ..." I take in a deep breath and huff it out as I lay my head back on the seat. "So when he asked for my number," I say and smirk when Z's eyes meet mine, "I gave him my ex's number. To piss two men off at the same time."

The low, deep rumble of Zander's laugh spreads a much-needed warmth through me. "That's one way to make an impression."

My smile is dull, but it's there. It lingers along with the grief that comes with the past.

"So you were always a smart-ass, stubborn woman?"

"You mean a bitch?" I question and Zander's quick to say, "I'd never call you that."

"Well, I would. I could be a bitch when I wanted to be one."

"I don't want you to call yourself that." His admonishment is a simple statement and as he turns the wheel, he has to remove his hand and along with it goes the warmth. Dom Z has returned it seems.

"Yes, Sir," I murmur sarcastically.

"Don't make me pull this car over and spank your ass because of your mouth." The warning on his lips changes the atmosphere of the car instantly.

His tone heats every nerve ending in my body at once. I wonder if he knows how much power he has over me.

"I'm sorry," I say and pull the hem of my black dress down. With my pulse quickened, I change the subject, back to Zander and Quincy.

"Do you have any stories?" I ask him.

"Stories of what?"

"Of you and Quincy."

He's quiet for a long moment, too long. An awkwardness

slips between us. "You don't have to tell me if you—" Just as I'm offering the both of us an out, he speaks up.

"I was drunk and wanted to pick a fight." He peeks over at me, smirking, and his hand returns to its rightful place on my thigh. "It also started at a bar."

His gentle smile picks up the corners of my lips. His jaw is strong, covered in a five o'clock shadow as I gauge his expression in profile.

"I was pissed. I'd gotten into a fight with my brother over our parents. He wanted them to go live with him. I wanted them to move down south where it was warm. It's what they wanted really."

"Why did they want to move?"

"Mom had chronic pneumonia and ... well, things had to change. Pops had a hard time taking care of everything although he wouldn't admit it."

"Did he love her?" My question throws Zander off and I almost feel compelled to explain myself. "I don't remember a time when my mother was alive, really ... only moments and they were fighting."

"Yeah," he says and nods, taking my hand in his and kissing my wrist before setting both our hands back down on my thigh. His thumb moves in soothing circles. "He loved her and she loved him."

"They're gone?"

He nods slowly and says, "Yeah, they had just passed. One

after the other and my brothers just made things worse."

"I'm sorry."

"You don't have to keep saying that, my little bird." I swear he almost says something else but stops himself. "She passed quickly. My father died later that year."

I have to bite down on my lip to keep from apologizing again. "How old were you?"

"Twenty-five. And angry."

"So you went to the bar," I say to remind him of the start of his story.

He sucks in a breath and nods. A moment later he has to turn the wheel again, but he makes do with just his one hand.

We're driving slower now and on a back road I'm not familiar with.

"I was angry at the world, but Cade got the most of it."

"Well ... if it's any consolation, Cade is an ass."

He chuckles. "Why do you say that?"

I shrug, shyness overcoming me. "Because I want to make you feel better."

This time he lets out a bark of a laugh and I love it. I love seeing this side of him. "You're sweet, Ella." His thumb taps, taps, taps as he pulls in the side entrance of a long lot with a row of brick buildings. At the very end is a larger building with parking all around it. I imagine that's the restaurant we're having dinner at.

"I wanted to pick a fight I guess, and she was there at the

end of the bar."

"Don't tell me you fought a woman," I say, dropping my voice to be comical.

He doesn't laugh. Instead he gives me a sad smile. "No, we didn't fight." His voice is hoarser but he keeps going. "She made me laugh. I hadn't laughed in a long time."

He stops then. Not speaking as we pull into a parking spot. The car sways slightly and he keeps it running as we sit there.

It hits me then, that he loved her. I thought he did when we were in the courtroom. He looked like a man who'd lost his love. Seeing him now, there's no question. He loved her.

"How long were you together?"

"About a year and a half." He doesn't hesitate. That little fact tells me more than anything.

"You loved her?"

He shakes his head once, but he doesn't speak. He doesn't say it out loud. "We were lovers."

My heart breaks in this small way watching him deny it. Suddenly I feel like a mistress, like an imposter posing on his arm. And I don't want it. Glancing at the restaurant and then back to the man denying the obvious, I no longer have much of an appetite.

"Did you come here with her?" I don't want to be here if that's the case.

"No. No, this place is new. But my friend suggested it."

He doesn't pick up on what's come over me, thankfully. I don't understand it fully myself and before I can think much of it, Zander kisses my knuckles.

"Thank you," he says between kisses and then stares deep into my eyes. "For coming with me today."

I melt for him, for the side of him he doesn't want to accept. The side that loves and breaks. The vulnerable bits that turn us crazy and allow us to fall into a well of emotion we can't control. I ache for him. Because I feel it. No one can deny the fact that I feel every bit of it. And then there are people like him, men who pretend they don't when it's so very obvious that they do.

I wonder if he would ever admit that he loved me. If he ever did fall for me. Would he say it? Would he tell me, or would I just have to know it and be complete with that?

"You're certain you want this?" he asks as he finally shuts off the car. "Knowing I'm a little fucked up too?"

"Yes."

"Show me," he commands and leans across the console of the car, taking my chin in his hand and kissing me deeply. So passionately it shocks me at first, my lips parted, granting him access and my world tilted. All because of him. Because of what he does to me.

Not a damn bit of it I can control.

CHAPTER 14

ZANDER

The days pass easily. It's been weeks now of spoiling Ella and enjoying her in bed ... as well as discovering her boundaries.

One thing I love is taking her out, and watching her light up a room when she doesn't even realize it.

Ella looks gorgeous in soft candlelight. She looks gorgeous in every light really, but the candlelight at the Italian restaurant does something special to her features. It catches in her silky hair and makes her dark, sultry eyes shine.

And it makes me want to do filthy things to her.

I feel lighter after the hearing, and somehow heavier. Lighter because this part of my history with Quincy is closed. There are no more hearings, other than the formal sentencing.

Heavier because I want Ella so much. My feelings seem much more intense than they should. Which makes me question them. More specifically if I'm using her emotionally because of what I went through with Quincy.

We go to dinner nearly every other night. Just like tonight.

She hasn't stopped talking since we got in the car, and only occasionally stops to take a drink and touch her throat. She's worlds better than she was only a month ago.

Tonight, she talks to me about surface-level things, things that don't hurt, things like what decor style she likes and how much of the garden she'd have to take out if she wanted to change the landscaping in her yard. It's a busy night and the waiter takes a few minutes to arrive.

It's all seemingly mundane, but the truth of the matter is that Ella's been discussing plans to redesign most of her home—never the blue room, though. She's told me repeatedly she loves that room as it is. Every plan she's made has fallen through. She ends up making some excuse as to why it isn't good enough and vetoes it all.

Damon mentioned it as well. It's a process, whether she realizes it or not. I'll be here through all of it.

Ella glances at her empty wineglass. It's late, getting later by the minute.

"Are you thinking about having a glass?" I ask her.

She readjusts the napkin on her lap. "No. Damon told me it's not the same when it mixes with the medication. It could make me feel lower than if I wasn't taking anything at all."

"Come here."

She listens. Of course she does. She's out of her seat in a heartbeat and sliding onto my side of the rounded booth a moment later. Close enough to touch, but not so close she's actually sitting in my lap, though I'd love that. I'd love so much with her.

I place my hand on her thigh. "Tell me more about the garden."

"Well—" Her cheeks flush, and she looks so beautiful against all this red fabric and the cream walls. All this dark wood and candlelight. "One of the beds is overgrown, so I'd probably have—"

I brush her dress up with the back of my hand, the silky deep red fabric gliding easily up her thigh, and Ella sucks in a little breath.

"Keep going," I command.

With her lips still parted and her voice breathy she whispers, "But I thought maybe a raised bed would be nice."

Another inch toward her waist, then another. It's entirely inappropriate. At the very last moment I slip my hand under the fabric and toy with the waistband of her panties. Her cheeks turn a deep rose. All the while, my focus is on the thin paper menu held in my left hand.

"You know what to say to stop this if it's too much," I murmur.

Ella bites her lip, and I dip under her panties to graze a knuckle against her softness and seek out her clit. She brings her hand up to cover her mouth, trying to make the movement seem natural, and I do it again.

"Good evening," the waiter greets us, and I feel her body stiffen. "Please forgive me for the wait. What can I get started for you tonight? Drinks?"

I don't take my hand away. I brush my knuckle over her clit as slowly as I've ever done it. "I'll have a cider. Whatever you recommend. Ella?"

I keep the pressure light, but I don't stop.

"I would—" Ella takes the drink menu in her hands, then lets it fall to the table. "A mocktail. Anything, really. Just something sweet."

A smile from the waiter. "I know the perfect thing."

He leaves, and I hold the menu in front of Ella while I play with her. She's hot, hotter than she's ever felt, and her breathing is shallow. "Have you done this before? Discreet play?"

She shakes her head. "The most outrageous thing I've ever done, you've probably seen. The ... swinging, recording, and uploading—"

"Exhibitionism." I add a little more pressure, cutting her off.

Ella gasps. "Yes—yes. We stopped when we got married." Discomfort presses out at the boundaries of my chest. I don't love hearing about her marriage before, but I won't order her not to talk about it. It's part of her past. It made her who she is today. "Our lifestyle changed. Our relationship changed."

"Do you miss it?"

I can tell how hard it is to follow the conversation against all the sensations. She's having to struggle to keep her ass on the seat instead of rocking into my fingers.

"I don't know what you mean, exactly." Dark eyes on mine. It's intense for her, and it's also intense for me. Her heat. Her closeness. The fact that I can't fuck her in this booth, as much as I want to. "Z," she begs me, her hands on mine, but I don't let up.

"The exhibitionism. Do you miss it?"

"I don't know."

I pretend to study the menu again. "What if something were to be leaked? Would that be upsetting? Exciting?" There's a low moan as she closes her eyes and reaches for her glass of water, but doesn't drink it.

"Little bird, I asked you a question."

A simper plays across her lips, and it takes most of my restraint not to push her down onto this booth and kiss her until she can't breathe. "I can't imagine anything being leaked that would be upsetting. It only excites me."

Goddamn. There isn't a part of me that's ever been intrigued by the fetish, until she refers to it as "exciting."

The waiter returns with my drink and something red and sugary in a martini glass for Ella. When he puts it down in front of her, I take my hand away.

"Oh," Ella says, clearing her throat and sounding so disappointed that my cock twitches. I can't help but to smirk.

"Would you like something else?" The waiter is genuinely concerned, his eyebrows knitting together. "I can get you anything else."

"No, no, no." Ella offers him an apologetic yet somehow bright smile. While he's still watching, still trying to gauge what was wrong, she sips it. "This is delicious."

I order my meal for the sole purpose that I know I'll be able to pick up a piece of the tagliata and slip it between her lips. The thinly sliced steak is simple, delicious, and I can already hear how she'll moan from the tender taste.

Ella orders next. All the while, Ella makes sure to give the waiter special attention. Beaming up at him. It would make me jealous if I didn't know she was only doing it to smooth things over. One thing I love about her is that she strives for those around her to be comfortable, her friends especially, but even people she'll only interact with once as well.

The waiter steps away, and as soon as he's out of earshot, Ella's eyes go wide and she scolds me in a whisper, "You stopped." How fucking adorable for my little submissive to show her disappointment.

"I did."

She pouts, that plump bottom lip tempting me to nip it.

"Did you think I would give you an orgasm before our food arrives? That would be too early into dinner, don't you think?"

I've never seen her face redder than it is right now.

With my forearms on the table, I lean over to speak directly into her ear. "You keep your thighs apart for me, jailbird. I'll tease you as long as you're good."

"Tease me?" Her voice is breathy. Oh, she can't hide how needy and desperate she is. Her eyes consider me for a moment, the reality sinking in. With her fingers toying with the napkin on her lap, she questions, "You're not going to let me come?"

"No."

The corners of Ella mouth turn up, almost as if she doesn't believe me. "I can't believe you'd do that. Tease me to the brink and leave me ..." she licks her lips, glancing away at the martini glass before concluding, "unwell."

I huff a laugh at her word of choice, but that's all she gets.

A bread basket arrives, dropped off by a passing server, and I wait until Ella has the first bite in her mouth before I touch her again. She's spread her legs under the table just like I told her to. She swallows the bread as I brush my fingertips over the softest part of her.

Petting her until her eyes go half-lidded.

"That bread must be fucking delicious," I tease her in a low groan. I'm hard as fuck watching her enjoy this without anyone else knowing. We're in a corner, and there's no one who can see. So long as I keep an eye out for the waiter.

Ella, in all her stubbornness, says nothing, merely rocking

into my touch.

"You're going to keep talking to me, jailbird. No matter what I'm doing to your clit."

"I think," she says, her voice breathy and light, "I'd like to visit a bookstore."

Her statement comes out of nowhere, and a quiet laugh leaves me. I don't stop, though, not my petting and not the conversation.

"Why's that?"

"I haven't replaced many of the books in the house in a long time. I don't want to feel like I'm living in a staged apartment." Her lips part as warmth rises to her cheeks and her eyes beg to shut so I drop my fingers lower, no longer concentrating on her most sensitive bundle.

With an exhale of relief, her shoulders drop and she reaches for her drink. "You know?"

"I don't know." Waiting for her to have a sip and place the glass down, I circle her clit, and her body tries to get more of my touch, which I deny her. "Your books aren't yours?"

"I don't have many on the shelves. I was into a more minimalist—a more minimalist design before. But now I think I'd like to read. What do you like to read?"

"I don't have a lot of time for it." Her eyes dance over my face. "I listen to music in the evenings, or podcasts. If I have time to read, I like science fiction and thrillers."

I stop touching her.

Ella bites her lip, but she doesn't push me on it again. She seems to sense the power between us. I'm controlling this, the way I do everything else. And I will reward her immensely for having the pleasure of teasing her like this.

"Good girl," I murmur into her ear, rewarding her with my hand back between her legs. "You're letting me play with you as much as I want. Following all the rules. You are being so good for me."

She lets out a shuddering sigh and when I dip down to her center, I find her hot and wet.

I toy with her all through dinner, and Ella turns down dessert when the waiter is still mid-sentence. Very much on edge and in need of getting the hell out of here and into bed. It's a good look on her. My insatiable smart-mouthed, yet obedient submissive.

Good. Because I'm wound tight too. I'm so fucking hard it hurts. I need her. I have to be careful when I stand, opting for discretion.

I escort her out of the restaurant with my hand on the small of her back. A stiff breeze greets us as we head toward the parking garage. Ella walks quickly, doing her best to keep up with my long strides. She's out of breath by the time we get to the third floor of the parking garage. "How do you do it?" she says as she hurries for the car. "How do you wait? Because I want you so much that I—"

"I'm done waiting."

I get one flash of relief in her dark eyes, and then I have my mouth on her. On her lips, and the side of her neck, and her collarbone. Fuck anyone who happens to walk up here. I've never experienced this desire Ella has, but I'll share it with her. A fast, hard fuck where someone could see. I'm careful as I push Ella's back against a concrete pillar, and she wraps her legs around me as if she's done it a thousand times. Hanging on tight while I deal with my zipper and push the fabric of her panties aside.

There's no mercy for her as I slam my cock to the hilt inside of her, knowing she's been ready for almost an hour now. "Fuck me," I groan in the crook of her neck. She feels like heaven.

Ella moans, her tightness enveloping me, her hips rocking back and forth. I've never felt anything this soft or sweet or hot, and I want to fuck her like this all night. The chill of the night wraps around us but it's no match for how warm and wet she is. I brace one hand against her ass and work the other between us to get to her clit.

"I'm not teasing this time," I growl into her ear. "Come for me."

She comes hard around me, squeezing tight, her cries echoing off the parking garage. The adrenaline rushes through my blood, my pulse racing. Nothing else matters in this moment except Ella.

CHAPTER 15

ELLA

The weeks pass in a blur. Every day checking off a list. Greeting Zander on my knees seems to be a favorite of his as time goes by. It's the first item on the slip of paper he gives me in the morning.

I love those moments.

The days, though … they come with ups and downs. Small moments where I feel so much lighter and then darker times where I close my eyes and remind myself: Grief is a ball in a box and it's okay.

The thoughts barely stay for long, because Zander's there or Damon. Even Kamden has been coming more frequently, making arrangements for me to attend different social events if I want to, all of them already approved by Zander and Damon.

They say I'm getting closer to a new normal, but almost every night, I glance down the hall no one talks about. When we lie together in bed, sometimes I forget and I think I'm in bed with James down the hall, being held and kissed and loved by him. Then I wake up, and it processes slowly.

I haven't told anyone. Not Damon, not Zander. Because if I said what I'm thinking, maybe they'd think I'm crazy. I think James wants me to go down the hall. I think he wants me to go back into our bedroom. Even if it's just to say goodbye.

Maybe he wants me to know that he's okay with everything that's happened. Maybe he's trying to tell me he still loves me, even if I'm in bed with another man. Maybe he wants me to know he misses me. Maybe it's all in my head.

The low rumble of an approaching thunderstorm drowns out the rustling of the trash bag at my side. It's easier to handle than the damn cardboard box I found in the garage, so I settled for it. The gray skies and increasing winds of the incoming downpour feel right for the occasion.

We loved the storms. One step at a time, one breath out and one in, I bypass the thin rope blocking off the west wing and flick on the light. Ignoring everything in front of me, I remember laying in James's arms on the porch of his uncle's house, under the tin roof, listening to the rain.

I can still hear him laugh as the bedroom door creaks open, the memories and the present moment colliding.

"One day we'll have a tin roof porch," he declared once. He

said it like a joke until I told him I'd love that. I love the storms.

The next exhale is more difficult, because it hurts even though it shouldn't. Simply existing shouldn't cause pain like it does when you're missing someone.

"You lied," I speak into the quiet room. It's colder in here. Unlike the hall, nothing in this room is covered. Roughly two years ago, I closed the door and told everyone not to enter it. And that's how it's remained. The heat clicks on as I drag my finger across the dresser. It's dusty and musty. I suppose that's what happens when a room is closed off for as long as this one has been.

With the trash bag still in my hand, I sit on the edge of the bed. It doesn't protest in the least. A thought crosses my mind that I didn't expect.

I wonder if Zander did this. If he cleaned out drawers he didn't want to ever open. I wonder if he had someone else clean up the traces of Quincy, the ones we're not supposed to leave around because it prevents us from "moving on."

I'd ask him, but just like this bedroom door was a moment ago, I think that conversation is a place Zander doesn't want to go. That it's something that's quite firmly locked up. Placing the bag on the bed, I focus on the other item that was balled up with it, the ancient phone that only texts.

I'm going to put some things aside.

It's odd to feel relief and accomplishment, sitting in a room, proud not to be losing it.

What? Kamden texts back. *What things? Do you need help?*

His messages come quickly, one after the other.

Let's just store them until I'm ready — My thumbs hesitate and I can't type the rest of the sentence so I hit send. The idea of typing, to get rid of them, disrupts the small moment of ease, the hope that I am strong enough for this.

I hope he doesn't ask, "Ready for what?"

Thankfully, he doesn't.

Okay. We can store anything you want for however long or indefinitely. Can I come over?

Staring down at his question, I don't know how to answer him. I think I want to be alone for this, but I don't know that I can be.

I have a meeting but I'll be done soon if you can wait.

No. The word is typed and sent before I can think twice about it. My breathing picks up as I push myself off the bed, taking in the abandoned room.

His texts don't stop and with each one, I know he doesn't trust me. He doesn't think I can do this. Insecurity weaves its way through me. *What about the girls? We'll make it a cozy night in—we can watch Hocus Pocus and Kelly can read our tarot cards?*

In an effort to reassure him, I tell him, *Damon knows.* I'm surprised by his response.

Where's Zander?

I lie and tell him, *Zander will be here soon.*

But where is he, did he tell you to do this?

No, it's just a part of me getting back to normal. It's such a lie to minimize it as a line on a checklist. But there's truth in it too. As my phone continues to vibrate with message after message, I pick up a silver frame from my old dresser. Sweeping off a thick layer of dust that clouds the photograph with my thumb, I peer down at a memory frozen in black and white. I used to call it "our photograph" because it's the one nearly every gossip column and media outlet used when it came out that we were seeing each other.

In the photo, I'm lying against his chest; I can still feel the stubble lining his chin that rested in the crook of my neck. His teeth are perfect and I remember joking with him that it could be an ad for a dentistry practice. We look happy. "We were so happy," I whisper to no one. Although my eyes gloss over, I hold it back and it's easier to do than I anticipated.

Kam continues texting and I let out a small laugh that surprises me. I'm not sure where it's come from, but I'll take the lightheartedness over the heaviness that's come over me.

I'm okay, Kam. I promise I'm okay.

If I text you every five minutes, will you be mad?

No ... I think I'd be okay with that.

Good. I'm here for you.

Through the parted curtains, I'm given a view of the storm raging on, the rain rampaging against the panes and a crack of lightning in the distance.

The frame makes a small clunk as I set it down and let out a heavy breath to steady myself. His clothes. I remind myself that it's not the furniture, it's not the visual reminders like that photograph, or anything like that that should be stored or donated. It's his clothes.

That's the only thing.

Naturally, I turn my back on his dresser and move to my nightstand. The lavender lotion is still there; picking it up, I find it's nearly full. A vision appears in front of me: the last time I remember using it. In silk pajamas with boy shorts and a matching tank top. I climbed into bed, under these sheets, and he was there, waiting for me.

I'm less careful dropping the lotion and then think it should be something that I toss in this bag, but I don't. Instead I spot the room spray from our honeymoon. I bought so many bottles of it but barely ever used it. Without touching it, the scent hits me as if bathed in it. The tropical scent of the Riviera Maya.

A sad smile crosses my face when I remember he told me I'd never use it. It was expensive and James couldn't have cared less. He was right, but he told me to get it, because it would make me happy.

It's not fair how many little things that are meaningless can bring on so much emotion.

Tears well again, but I hold them back, forcing myself to

open just one drawer and get it over with. Just one drawer, clothes that should be donated. Clothes that I don't need to hold on to anymore.

The lightning strikes closer, and there's a louder rumble this time. The rain beats down as the drawer scrapes open. It's a long drawer and I get down on my knees to go through the few pieces that lay in the bottom.

There aren't many pieces at all. This was our vacation home. We were barely here, so it shouldn't be surprising but somehow it is.

The first three garments are easy. I toss the shorts and jeans into the bag and I'm able to go through the entire drawer. There's nothing to keep. Nothing that should stay here.

Sitting on my heels, I lean back and look at the pathetically empty bag and then open the next drawer and the next.

It seems easier and easier as the rain pours down and the lightning lessens, until I get to one piece. One rugby shirt that I hated. God, it looked awful on him. The fit was all wrong, the fabric too thick. I never hated a shirt more.

The storm carries on as I hold up the orange shirt, still not seeing the appeal. I remember how he laughed about how much I hated it. I'm surprised to even see it here. Just as I'm thinking he never wore it, or at least I don't remember him ever wearing it, I see the tags.

It's brand new. He had it for years and never wore it.

"You're not wearing that. It's awful."

"You're a little small to be so bossy," he joked, *smiling down at me.*

"Seriously, I'll dye my hair if you put that thing on."

The moment takes over, his hands on me, how he backed me up against the wall.

I don't realize I'm crying, hot wet lines running down my face, until my phone goes off with a text.

Laying the shirt on my lap but not letting it go, I answer the phone with my other hand and see I've missed three texts from Kamden.

You okay?

Hey babe I just need you to message me, okay?

Please, Ella. I'm a PITA but I love you and anything will do.

As I'm reading them, another comes through. *Don't be mad, I messaged Damon.*

Shifting so my ass is on the floor, I let the shirt go and respond. *I'm here. Just had a moment.* It's not so ladylike as I wipe under my nose and consider using the damn shirt as a tissue. A small laugh leaves me at the thought, but then without warning, I sob. Crying into the shirt with fresh hot tears.

"Oh my fucking God what is wrong with me," I murmur in between wiping at my face with the shirt. *Feel it and let it go.*

Even as I tell myself to let go of the emotions, I don't want to let go of the shirt. I don't know that I'm ready. I don't think I'm ready.

Focusing on my breathing, I quickly text, *Kam I don't think I'm ready to throw anything away.*

That's okay, that's totally fine.

My fingers fly across the keys. *I mean the houses too. I don't want anyone to touch them.*

Even as I send them, I know it's unreasonable. I know it is. I just want to stay still for a moment. I'm just not ready for it to change.

I text him again adding, *Please*, but I can't explain why.

I spend too long staring down at the rumpled trash bag and wrinkled-up shirt, with my hands trembling. It's not until Kam tells me no one will touch anything and that he'll make sure of it that I'm able to consider pulling myself together.

Shame creeps up my spine at how easy it was for me to fall apart.

I couldn't clear out a dresser of clothes.

"Ella." Zander's voice carries through from the cracked bedroom door. It creaks open; he doesn't wait for me to answer.

I'm sure I'm a sight to behold. There's no doubt my mascara has run, my cheeks are tearstained and I'm sure my nose is red. Taking in a steadying breath, I slowly rise to my feet, not bothering to hide anything at all.

"Ella," he repeats, saying my name with a gentleness, a comfort that's unexpected. I suck in a deep breath, meant to make it all right, but instead my expression crumples and my throat goes tight. He's quick to wrap his arms around me, bringing me back down to the ground, nestled in his lap as I cling to his shirt. I fist his cotton T-shirt, burying my head in his chest.

One deep breath after the other as he shushes me, rubbing soothing circles on my back and rocking me slightly. Back and forth as the waves of chaotic grieving dim.

With my eyes closed, I breathe Zander in, his unique scent. It's masculine but clean. Like fresh open water.

"I thought I was doing good," I whisper, opening my eyes to see the light shining off the silver frame. My gaze drops until Zander grips my chin between his thumb and forefinger, bringing my eyes up to his.

The world pauses. All my thoughts, all the sorrow just as much as the battering of the rain when he traps me with his emerald and amber eyes. He doesn't see through me, he sees all of me. Every last piece and I can't breathe.

"You did very well and I'm proud of you." He's the one to close his eyes and when his lips meet mine, I close mine too. His kiss is bruising, taking without remorse and consuming me in a way I'd forgotten I could feel.

The only way I can think to describe it is safe, cherished, wanted ... I don't know that any one word is enough. It feels like it'll be okay. Maybe even that nothing else matters. As long as I just stay right here.

He lowers his head again and my eyes close, eager for him to do that again. To make it all go away. To make me his and nothing but that.

My lips mold to his until he nips my bottom lip. A gasp leaves me at the sudden hint of pain.

"Good girl," he whispers against my lips and then kisses my forehead.

I hadn't realized how tired I was until I rest my cheek on his chest.

"Did I interrupt you?" he questions.

A knot forms in my chest and I readjust to sit up, to feel the cool air against my heated face. "I think I did all I should for today."

I peek up at Zander to find him considering the bag of clothes. He doesn't question anything, he only nods and then pushes the drawer shut to lean against the dresser, keeping his arm around his waist to pull me along with him.

With his legs bent on either side of me, both arms wrapped around me and my head resting against his shoulder, he sits with me, in this room that doesn't belong to either of us.

It belongs to what once was.

My exhale shudders out of me. Unsteady and daring me to let my thoughts wander.

"You came in with a purpose. I will stay until you've done what you wanted." I tilt my head back to peer up at Zander, who takes his time to look back down at me.

"What are you going to do? Follow me from room to room?" I don't hide the incredulousness from my tone.

His answer is as simple as it is definitive. "If that's what you need."

"You have more important things to do than to babysit me."

"No, Ella, I don't."

For the second time in only moments, I feel caught, but safe. Seen and protected. All at once, it's suffocating and I tear my gaze from his. Staring across the room, I tell him, "I had planned to do one drawer."

"It looks like you did that."

I can only nod, my snide thoughts telling me I should have stopped while I was ahead. "I did."

"Next time I'd like you to tell me." His strong hand wraps around my thigh. "Poor Damon was standing outside of the door not knowing what to do with himself."

Surprised, I turn to face Zander, who grins at my shock.

"No he wasn't."

He laughs slightly, his broad chest shaking as he does. He nods and tells me, "He was."

Brushing at my knee, I stare at the thick accent rug, feeling guilty. "I didn't mean to make him worry."

"We can't help but worry," he tells me. His thumb runs along my cheek, as if he's brushing away tears that no longer exist. "I want to be here for you. Don't deprive me of that, my little bird."

My heart thumps, loud and heavy. Refusing to go unnoticed. Three words nearly slip from my lips, reckless and nothing but raw emotion. The moment I catch them, I swallow them down. I haven't forgotten Damon's comment about displacing my feelings.

Zander stands slowly, holding his hand out for me. "Come." He towers over me.

There's a question that lingers, that begs to be spoken. Asking if we'll ever be more. With my small hand in his, I consider asking him, letting it out and seeing where the chips may fall.

"You did well today. I'm proud of you," he tells me. Like a Dom speaks to his submissive. Matter of fact.

"Thank you," I whisper and the chill of the room creeps over my shoulders.

The question goes unasked. We've both already loved. I'll never be the woman he met in the bar who made him laugh. And he'll never be the man who wanted me so desperately that he wouldn't take no for an answer.

He's only my Dom. And to him, I am only his submissive.

It's only when we're leaving, the bag and rumpled rugby shirt staying where they are, that I notice the rain has stopped.

CHAPTER 16

ZANDER

Ella's doing well. The sessions with Damon, the new coping habits—all of it is everything I could have hoped for when The Firm took over her care. But something makes me suspicious. Like it's going too well.

Like she might be hiding something, or burying something. Separating from me in a way I don't like. But then, of course, that's the whole point. That Ella will grow to a place where she doesn't need any of us anymore.

Except ... I want her to need me. The way I'm coming to need her. Or maybe it's only a powerful desire.

I am so fucking conflicted with her. She's still grieving and I have no idea what she truly wants. A Dom or more. Let alone what she's capable of committing to once her life goes back to what it was.

We're in her sitting room in the middle of all that blue, and I can't keep my eyes off her. Ella is curled into a chair with a book on her lap, and all I can do is sit here and stare at her. Marveling at her progress but hesitant to let my guard down.

It's a cold, dreary day. We could spend days like this in a hundred different ways. Like in my dungeon, for instance. I want to show it to her, but I don't know if she'd approve.

It's one thing to have this relationship in the comfort of her home. It's another to pluck her away and toy with her like I truly want to do.

I don't know if it would meet her standards. Ella's house is a testament to her wealth. She's swimming in it. Drowning in it. Would she even accept the lifestyle I want? I don't realize I've started looking out the window at the thrashing trees until she speaks.

"Z?"

"Yeah?"

A hint of worry in her dark eyes. "Would you hold me?"

I open my arms to her, and she drops the book to come to me. Her only stop is by the fireplace to hit the switch. It springs to life in the grate, filling the space with orange flames, and Ella crawls into my lap. It'll be winter soon. The snow will blanket us in. It's different from my place in Pennsylvania. Everything is different here, and I'm not sure how the two worlds fit together. I'm not sure if they can.

It's all going well, but can this be sustained?

Ella rests her head on my shoulder, and I tuck a blanket around her on my lap. There. This is the way to sit in silence together. With her so close I can feel her heat.

Hypothetically, how would I live without her? I can't exactly picture her in my house in lower Pennsylvania. It's significantly smaller than her place. Substantially less in nearly every way and I have never wanted to live in a home that feels ... expansive and impersonal. My home doesn't have a separate sitting room and a rec room and an enormous backyard. It doesn't come with gardening staff and people to take out the flower beds if you want them redone. Ella lives in a world surrounded by people to support her, care for her, and work for her. It would just be me in Pennsylvania. I don't have any desire for this life.

I can't even be sure I'd be with The Firm anymore, and I have to question myself—really question myself—about whether my desire for Ella is pure desire for her or if it's strengthened by the fact that I've given up my job for her. For a long time, The Firm was the steadiest thing in my life. The jobs we took under my brother's direction provided a shape to my days, a way to make good money, and a reason to get up in the morning.

I'm not questioning if Ella would be enough. She would be—I know that by the way she fits into my arms. By the way her scent makes me feel, which is powerful and peaceful at the same time. But would I be enough for her, if I told her I didn't want this?

I breathe through the thoughts in my head. They are just thoughts, and having them doesn't make any one of them truer than the others. I hold my emotions at a distance and try to consider them with an impartial mind. I'm obviously unsettled about how things have been left with The Firm. I'm wishing for more solid footing in my life, and not having it is causing some fear and anxiety. But mostly, overriding everything, is how much I want Ella. How much I care for her. I can't keep that feeling at any kind of distance. It's too close.

"Would you ever want to live with me? To continue our power exchange in my home, rather than here?"

Her head comes up, curiosity running through the shades of amber in her dark eyes. "Yes."

"Even if it wasn't all of this?" I gesture around us and the obvious wealth. "I can take care of you, but this is not a lifestyle I ever imagined for myself."

She pushes herself up to look into my eyes. "Would you ever want to live with me, then? Even if it *was* all this?"

I smirk at her to cover the instant twinge of uncertainty that burrows into my gut. "I don't think I could maintain this lifestyle for you."

"You wouldn't have to. I've never had to work a day in my life. When my father died, I got everything. There wasn't anyone else to inherit a thing. Even his business partners and everyone else suing for this and that and claiming rights ..." She lies back down, as if comforted by the memory and explains, "Kam took down every single one of them and I got every dime to my father's name."

There's something ... off about the manner in which she delivered that statement. Like she's used to the vultures, used to litigation.

"Did you expect that? That when he died, you'd have to fight to keep what he left you?"

There's a sad smile that graces her lips as she peers into the fire. "In this world, there is always someone wanting what's yours. I remember once, I ..." she hesitates and I tell her to go on, to tell me what she's thinking.

Swallowing thickly she admits, "Kelly, Trish and I, we were as thick as thieves."

"You still are from what I can tell."

Her hair rustles against my chest as she readjusts in my lap, getting more comfortable, still staring at the fire as if it's playing back her memories. "We are. Because of the shit we got into. Drugs, alcohol ... we were given invitations that no one should ever give minors. And I didn't have a father or mother to tell me no. I had Kamden. Who was used to getting himself and his sister out of trouble."

"I've seen your record."

"It's a colorful résumé, isn't it?" she sighs, not with nostalgia, but with regret. "I'm thankful for Kam and what he did for me. If it weren't for him, I might not be this version of fucked up, but I would be a hollow shell of ..." She breathes in deeply before clearing her throat. "What I mean is that, all of this, is forever mine. There's no needing support from anyone. So if you could want this, then it's no bother."

"I imagine—this—comes with Kam? Kamden was there for everything?"

"Always." Ella skims her finger over the collar of my shirt. "Ever since I can remember. Our families have known each other forever. You know Kam's sister, Trish and I, we got along from the start. That's the way it is in this life. There are so very few people you can trust. You tend to stick with the ones you know, and we always knew Kam's."

I had friends growing up, though none were wealthy and there was never a threat of trusting the wrong person. Family friends, of course. My family had those. But they came and went and came back. It was easy. Society fears were never something I concerned myself with.

"Why did you choose him to take custody of you back then? When your father died and you were sixteen." I'm surprised by the spike of needless jealousy. I can't go back in time to be in every part of Ella's life, as much as I want to. And even if I could, I don't know if I'd do it. The way Ella and I are together is only possible because of the people we are right now, and those people were shaped by the past.

She frowns, her eyes going distant. "I knew he'd do

anything for me. He took care of ... a lot of things. So it made sense."

In the space of this one sentence, her tone has changed. It's off, and her body stiffens in my arm.

"Don't withdraw from me, jailbird. We're in this conversation until it's over, unless you want to use your safe word."

Her eyebrows go up as color darkens her cheeks. "I can safe word out of a conversation?"

"You can use your safe word at any time," I remind her. "It's not just for when I'm fucking you, or when you're bound. It's for any time. Because our relationship is twenty-four seven, so is your safe word. Do you feel like you might need to use it?"

Ella considers it for a moment, like she should. I'm proud of her for not immediately saying no. Some submissives become convinced that using the safe word is a kind of weakness, and that it makes their Doms happier if they don't use it. That's not the case at all. I need her to know she can use her safe word at any point, because otherwise I can't adjust my methods. It's crucial to be comfortable with using a safe word. I've always thought that a reluctance to use it is a sign that the Dom hasn't done his job. I'm going to do well by Ella. I won't let her down.

"No. I don't need to use it." She takes a deep breath, steadying herself. "When he died—my father, I mean—there were a number of people in my life I didn't trust. I knew I could trust Kam."

"How did you know you could trust him?"

"He knew things I'd done. And he knew things about my father. He knew everything." Ella swallows, meeting my eyes. "You can trust someone who knows all your darkest secrets. You know?"

CHAPTER 17

ELLA

There is purpose in suffering. Damon's previous declaration has wreaked havoc on me since I woke up in the middle of the night and struggled to get back to sleep. With my eyes feeling heavy, the questions roll around in the back of my mind.

What the fuck purpose is worth what I went through? The tragedies that so many people endure have purpose?

The question sticks to my tongue as Damon takes his seat on the patio chair across from where I'm lying. In high-waisted jeans and a cream sweater, I don't have to worry about covering anything from him.

"Enjoying the fire without me?" he jokes, leaning back in the chair. The fire burns bright behind him. Damon's gotten back to his more casual, friendly banter with me. Any bit of tension or uncertainty since The Firm found out about Zander and I has subsided entirely.

But why would he tell me there is purpose in suffering? The more I think about it, the more it almost seems cruel. The question is still there, but I swallow it and answer, "It's the perfect day for the fireplace out here, don't you think?"

"There's a nice chill out here, I'll admit."

What purpose could be worth *this*? I've been thinking about it all day. He said there was purpose in suffering, but what could possibly be worth the suffering that comes with loss?

"Something on your mind?" he questions and I run my teeth along my lower lip, considering him.

"Did Z send you out here to babysit me while he left?"

With a shake of his head, Damon crosses his ankle to his other knee.

"You look like a therapist, you know that?" I point with a chipped nail and add, "Especially in a collared shirt under that sweater."

"You sound like a patient avoiding meaningful conversation."

I huff out a laugh and ask, "What's it called when you keep thinking about the same thing over and over?"

"Obsessing?"

"No." I'm quick to dismiss that suggestion. "When it's things that make you sad."

He nods and says, "Ruminating. Excessive thinking about negative feelings."

Snapping my fingers, I point at him and say, "That's the one."

"What are you thinking about?" he questions but then corrects himself. "What can't you stop thinking about?"

I watch his foot tap on nothing in the air.

"Missing James," I confess under my breath and I let my expression show the sadness I've been concealing as I add, "Don't tell him. Please."

"Zander?"

Swallowing thickly, I nod.

"He knows that you miss him. But I won't tell him anything in our conversations. It's only between the two of us."

"I can't stop thinking about how if James had looked, even though he had the right-of-way, or if I'd seen it quicker and yelled."

"That must feel heavy."

I murmur without looking back at him, "Endless loop about my current suffering."

"I have to be honest." He waits for me to peek up at him before he tells me, "I'm not a fan of that loop of yours." He offers me a kind smile and raises his brow.

"That would make two of us."

"But I'm happy that you're talking about it."

"I want it to stop," I confess to him, not hearing whatever

he's just said. "How do you make it stop?" The question reeks of desperation.

"Recognize that you are ruminating. Acknowledging that it's not productive."

"I do that. When I go there, I realize it's happening at least."

"Good. Good."

"And then I'm angry that I'm thinking about it again and reliving it. I get so frustrated with myself ... it doesn't stop."

"I need you to know that we are not our thoughts. Separate the feelings from the thoughts."

"I thought you said there was purpose in suffering." The words race out of me, nearly sounding accusatory.

"The purpose of suffering is not *to* suffer. The purpose is knowing why you feel that way and then what you can do, if you can do anything. In your case, you can't."

"I wish I could."

"That's understandable."

"Help me make it stop," I practically beg him, praying he can understand how much it still hurts. "Please."

"Tell yourself it's just a ball in a box. The button was pushed. Was there something that led to it or not? If there's nothing to do, nothing to control, let it go."

"Okay. Let it go."

Damon makes a show of looking at his watch. "Well, we dove right in, didn't we?"

I let out a small laugh, laying back into the pillow.

"Do you know what triggered it?"

The bedroom. I don't answer him, though. "I think I'd rather talk about something else."

"We can do that."

My lips perk up into a soft smile. "You're easy to talk to, you know that?" Damon's broad smile is comforting. I add, "And you have a beautiful smile."

"Well, now you're just buttering me up for something."

I don't say anything, I return my attention to the lone loose thread on the knee of my jeans. *Just let it go. Feel it and let it go.* The advice resonates but it's too simple. At this moment, I'm not sure how to feel about its simplicity.

"If you don't want to talk about James, maybe we can talk about Zander?" Damon suggests.

"What about him?"

"Have your other relationships been similar? Romantically or sexually?"

"As in, have I had other Doms in my life?"

Damon nods.

"Only one. My husband. But it wasn't the same."

"Do you want to talk about it?"

I shift again, feeling colder as the breeze sweeps my hair in front of my face. "I ... feel uncomfortable comparing the two of them."

"Remember that it's okay to be uncomfortable. There are no good or bad emotions. Only comfortable and uncomfortable, and there's nothing wrong with either."

"I don't want to talk about him right now."

"I understand. Let's go back a bit, shall we?"

Nodding, I clear my throat. "Okay."

"Back on the topic of sex, sexual empowerment, is that what you called it?" He references a conversation we had the other day.

"Yes."

"You said something about having all the money in the world, but you choose to use your platform for sexual empowerment."

"My social media following." Yesterday and the day before, I went on little rants mostly. Apparently Damon wants to hear more of my "I am woman, hear me roar" movement.

"That's right."

"How far back did you go when you looked through my social media posts?" I question him nearly comically, although it doesn't reflect in my expression or tone.

"To the beginning, skimming," he admits which is shocking. "I wanted to make sure I understood what you meant about using your platform for empowering women and sex positivity."

"Being called a whore and slut for years will do it, I guess." Those types of comments started the moment I wore my first bikini ... I think I was fourteen. I know my dad was still alive, so I was young, just posing with friends at the beach.

"I did notice when you got engaged so did the amount of overt expression in your posts."

"I like posting things that make women more comfortable with their bodies and sexuality. I always have but I had to be careful. I didn't want to sound bitchy or judgy ... I just wanted women to know it was okay to want sex. To have sex. To wear what they want and to say no if they didn't want to do something. That it didn't make them "less than" to want some *activities*."

"Was your mother an active role or voice in that subject?"

My snort is exceptionally unladylike. "No. No, not at all. I don't remember much about my mother except ..."

"Except what?"

"Fighting."

A cool breeze blows by and I emphasize, "They were *always* yelling."

"You were young when your mother died, but you remember them fighting?"

"There are very few memories I have of her," I tell him and moments flash in my mind. "In nearly all of them, she was fighting with my father."

"Do you want to talk about what happened with your mother?"

"You know what happened." My blood chills and the sun starts to set, dimming the natural light far too quickly.

"Are their deaths, the trial, their fighting something you

think about often?"

Staring blankly at him, I wish I could speak as easily as I just have when talking about my upbringing.

"Do you remember how you felt during those harder times?" Suddenly the topic of sex no longer seems important. Damon watches me like he's gotten to something he'd like to dig up.

The screaming is what I remember most. I'd wake up from them screaming at each other. "Scared, angry ... like any child would be." With another breeze blowing, I brush my hair from out of my face and cross my arms.

"Guarded?" Damon pokes fun and I tsk him. "It's just cold." My heart does a little tap in my chest that's uneven. Yes. This conversation makes me very guarded and I wonder if Damon saw posts or comments that he shouldn't have. Kam said they were all removed.

"Did it ever get physical?"

"Yes." I nod, my throat going tight and dry. "I can still remember the sound of him slapping her so hard she fell to the ground."

The tapping in my chest continues, intensifying and quickening when he asks, "Do you remember how old you were?"

"I had to be in middle school."

"I imagine that was difficult."

Enough. Enough. We're not supposed to be talking about

this. "I don't see how any of this relates to anything at all."

"Conflict resolution is a learned behavior. How did you learn to handle your emotions when you were dealt such severe ones at a young age? You just told me you know that you're ruminating, but don't know how to stop. You've told me a number of stories where you struggle with your emotions."

"I think that's normal."

"Just because it's normal doesn't mean it's healthy. I want to help you, so tell me."

"Tell you what?"

"What happened when they fought?'

With a deep breath in, I answer him, "That's something I haven't thought about in a while." He starts to say something, but I cut him off. "You know how we started this conversation with ruminating? I used to stay up at night, thinking about their fights and if I could change anything."

"And how did you cope with those feelings?" he questions and the events play in my head. Kelly, Trish and Kam ... the plan. Uncovering the truth and then covering it all back up. How did I cope? I did something I shouldn't have.

"I think we should go inside," I whisper.

CHAPTER 18

ZANDER

The two of them are sitting in the blue room in front of the fire, and I know right away that the session has pushed Ella to one of her boundaries. Or to a place where she needs someone else to act as a boundary for her. She needs me. Her face is pale, and her eyes shine, but she's not crying. I pull a chair directly in front of her so I can take her hands in mine and look her in the eye. Damon watches from his seat, his face neutral.

"What's wrong?"

Damon begins to answer. "Ella and I were discussing her past with her—"

"Wait, Damon. Quiet." My tone wasn't meant to come out the way it did. "Please," I add for good measure. "I want

Ella to tell me what happened." I stroke a lock of hair away from her cheek.

Her only acknowledgement is to scoot on the sofa and make room for me to sit next to her. There's a sadness that doesn't leave her gaze, which flicks between the mine and the fire.

"She has a voice, and I want her to use it. Tell me." She knows a command when she hears one, and her body settles into the sofa a bit.

"There's a lot," she admits, and her voice is soft and slightly shaken. "I have a lot of memories. Some of them I wish I could forget ... and today," she pauses to take in an unsteady breath, "I'm just remembering a lot right now."

"We're going to go over them now, in a safe place." I don't want to push her past what she can take, but because Ella is a submissive, I make the decision for her. She still holds the power over the conversation. She can use her safe word at any time. "I'm listening."

"James—" Ella lifts her chin a fraction of an inch. "James knew about it. He knew about what happened, and I wish—" Now her eyes brim with tears.

It's obvious how difficult it is for her, and I've never wished for anything more than I wish she didn't have to remember these things. I wish she had a clean slate, and that her life had been the fairy tale she deserves. "I wish you already knew so I didn't have to say it out loud."

"You will say it out loud, and I'll hear it, and then I'll know," I reassure her. "It won't have so much power over you once you've told me." I hope it's true for Ella. I kept what happened with Quincy bottled up from as many people as possible, but it all had to come out eventually. Otherwise I couldn't have survived it. The longer you let a secret fester, the worse it gets.

Ella takes a shaky breath, and I run my thumb over the back of her hand. "My father abused my mother. He—he beat her. Not just once or twice, Z."

"And you saw?"

"Yes. I saw it. And it didn't seem to matter if anyone knew. He knew I saw, and that only seemed to make it worse. If he caught me looking, he would make it worse for her." Tears spill down Ella's cheeks. "Watching was dangerous, and so ..."

"So what? What were you going to say?"

"I don't know. I like people to know, I like them to see what's really there. I want them to know it all ... and see it all."

"I'm not sure this is—" Damon pipes up and makes his hesitation known. Whatever conclusion Ella's come to, he doesn't necessarily agree with.

"So maybe with James and other men, I liked for people to see me. It's wrong to even talk about those things one after the other—"

"It's not wrong," I say, cutting off that line of thinking, although I'm still not entirely sure what she means.

"I think I like people to see and hear it all, because I wish they knew everything I knew back then. So ranting about what's on my mind ... fucking whoever I want on camera, whatever it is, I want them all to see it. They're going to judge me anyway, so let the facts of my judgment be crystal clear and out there in the world for all to see."

"Each part of your life affects every other part. If being a witness was wrong in your childhood, then being witnessed can be a way to take back your control over that. It's okay, jailbird."

The name slips out before I can stop it, but Damon says nothing. I'm going to have to ask Kam about all this shit. This is much darker than I thought it would be. Than I ever imagined for Ella.

"Maybe I wanted to be seen back then, because it wasn't dangerous with James."

"Do you think it would be dangerous to be seen with me?"

"I don't know." She doesn't take her eyes off my face. Doesn't glance in Damon's direction. But the color has come back to her face and she leans closer to me, her breath quickening with anticipation. "I want to feel powerful enough to show everyone what really happens," she whispers. "I want them to see what my life is really like."

I take her face in my hands and pull her in for a kiss. Hard. Deep. Like I don't give a fuck if Damon is sitting there. The truth is that I don't. If Ella wants power, I have one way to hand it to her—by taking it from her. That's the game we play, at its core.

With tearstained cheeks she peers up at me through her thick lashes and murmurs, "Do you still want me? Even if I'm this fucked up?"

There isn't a second I hesitate. I stand her up between my knees and strip off her jeans and panties together at once, consumed with her body. With the delicate, elegant frame under a soft baggy sweater. It means that even when she's naked below the waist, she's still partially covered. Ella reaches for me over and over, not wanting to break the kiss. I let her kiss me for as long as I can stand it, and then I push her back into the sofa. I know Damon's seated in a dark blue armchair behind us, and the angle in relation to Damon will keep her partially out of view.

But not entirely. My heart rages in my chest, wanting her to know I want her all the more for confiding in me. More than I care about anything else.

He still hasn't moved, and I know he's not going to. If he wanted out of this, he could have gotten up at any time. Still can.

Either way, I'm going to fuck Ella exactly how she wants to be fucked.

I spread her thighs to the edge of the chair. Her chest rises faster, and I slide my hands between her thighs and lean in close. It's only an illusion that we're having a private conversation. Damon can hear every word. But I do it anyway. "You can use your safe word at any time."

Ella gives the tiniest nod of her head. Her breathing is slower and heavier.

"He can see you," I tell her.

She takes in a quiet gasp, her head tipping back against the chair, and I can feel how much she wants this. Her thighs are already trembling beneath my palms.

It only takes one movement to switch places with her. Pull her out of her seat, take her place, and pull her into my lap. I undo my pants as soon as I'm underneath her, gripping my cock and use my hands on her hips to guide her down. Ella reaches for my shoulders, her cheeks reddened. She lets out a small moan as the head of my cock meets her opening and I pull her down hard.

The gasp she gives me, with her lips parted and her eyes wide, is fucking everything.

Her pussy is wet for me, and the only resistance she offers is that she's so tight. I curse softly into her ear as she buries her face in my shoulder and rides me. I'm going to keep her moving, keep her fucking me with the rhythm I want. She wants this too. She wants it so much that she can't relax into my hands. Ella's hips move faster in my grip. Almost frenzied.

In a quick glance, I note that Damon hasn't left.

"He's still looking," I whisper at the shell of Ella's ear. "He's watching while you fuck me. Do you wish you knew how much he could see, jailbird?"

She doesn't answer me; instead she struggles to say, "I'm going to—" Her pussy clenches, and I know. It happens again and again, the pace picking up. "I'm going to come—"

"Good girl. Come for me."

Ella's orgasm is a pretty, shuddering thing, her face hot on my neck and her hands fisted in my shirt.

When she moves to slow down, I stop her. I'll lift her up and down myself if I have to. "You're not done, jailbird. Not until I am. Keep going."

All's quiet at Ella's house the next morning, except for the sputtering of a coffee pot. She's still sleeping when Damon comes in through the back door for his shift.

When I was done with Ella, Damon had left and Silas was in the rec room, his shift having started. I messaged him a number of times, dancing around the obvious.

I'm at the countertop with a cup of coffee in my hand, and when he sees me, he cocks a brow, closing the sliding door with one hand. I wish I could say I didn't feel the heat of slight embarrassment.

"Morning," I tell him.

"Morning to you too." The awkwardness is only slight.

"About last night ..." I start and he finishes.

"I figure I won't address it unless she needs to be reassured that there is no judgment from me?"

I'm slow to nod, considering his expression.

"Her coping mechanisms are," he says and breathes in, "apparently compatible with yours." The grin against his cleanly shaven face is humorous. I huff a laugh, picking up the mug to take a drink.

"Apparently so."

"Do you think she'll need reassurance?" he questions in a more serious tone.

I consider him, and the situation before answering. "I think she needs more reassurance that it was all right to cry, more so than anything else. I think she needs to know that whatever happened back then, is okay to put in the past."

Damon nods, pulling a stool out from the counter to sit beside me. "So, listen. I did some research last night on Ella's father like you asked me to."

"Did you find anything that could be helpful?"

"There were some records of her father's abuse, all sealed and don't ask me how I got them."

I nod and tell him, "I won't ask Silas either."

"Good. But the records only contained statements and evidence of his abuse toward his first wife, not his second. She tried to press charges once, but they were dismissed on the grounds that she was mentally ill and filed a false report. When she died by suicide, no one questioned it at first."

"Suicide? I thought—"

"Evidence came to light years later on that. The allegations that Ella's mother was responsible. It wasn't suicide, it was murder."

"Do you have the records of what the evidence was?"

Damon nods his head. "I can send you the file, but keep it to yourself." He meets my eye. "It was also sealed and it looks like ..." He struggles with what to say next. "Whoever sealed it didn't want it found, is all I'm going to say."

"So whatever he did to his first wife, he might have done to the second?"

"Potentially, although she never hinted at abuse herself and she certainly had a reason to speak up when she was tried for murder. She also ... died by suicide in her cell before the trial was over."

"Suicide. Ella's mother committed suicide. Do you think there's a genetic—"

"Ella's on antidepressants. But more than that ... with what's in that file, I would be surprised if her mother really killed herself."

My friend shrugs off his jacket, getting off his stool to hang it up by the door. "The court cases mostly focused on Ella, from what I can see. It's like she was used as a distraction in some ways."

"To garner sympathy for her mother?"

"No." He frowns. "Sympathy for her father."

"That's ... interesting."

"Everything that's documented is odd. Half of it doesn't appear to even appear to be legally relevant."

My gut churns. "How old was Ella?"

"The trial lasted two years and started when Ella was only seven."

Damon grabs a mug and gets his own cup of coffee, stirring in some sugar. Then he goes to the fridge and adds milk before coming back and taking his seat. "Cases involving the wealthy are generally pretty calculated." He tests his coffee, then looks over the mug at me.

"Anyway, I thought I should mention it since you asked me to look into ... whether he'd hurt Ella or not, or rather the extent of it."

"What do you think?"

"I wouldn't put it past him."

The air turns stale between us as we each drink in silence. Glancing at my phone, I turn on the security app and check to see Ella, still sleeping soundly in bed.

"You're not supposed to have that anymore."

I peek up to find Damon tipping his coffee mug toward me.

"Do me a favor, and pretend like you didn't see."

He doesn't respond to that request, although he doesn't comment on it anymore either. "How are things going between you and Ella?"

Damon did just watch us fuck last night, I contemplate

reminding him just to fuck with him. But there's more to it and we both know that. I don't know what to tell him. I have feelings for her. Obviously I do. But I've also been gentle with her, too much perhaps. I'm aware that she's still grieving and coping with things that have happened to her as well as how she's handled them. It's heavy. With her, it feels easy, but everything surrounding us is troubled.

"She said she'd live with me," I tell him.

His brow shoots up higher than they did when he first walked in. The surprise is genuine on Damon's face. "You're moving in together?"

"Only under the parameters of our current relationship. And we also hadn't exactly decided one way or another on where we'd live."

He snorts, almost spilling his coffee in the process. "What are the parameters?" He uses one hand to make air quotes around parameters. "That you'll just have your power exchange and never ever fall for each other?" There's an air of sarcasm that coats his guess.

"Something like that."

"Bullshit. You and Ella, moving in together, and it's not something more? I don't buy that for a second, Zander. You're really going to try to pull one over on me?"

"I'm not pulling anything over on you. That's all we talked about. We didn't talk about a romantic relationship. We're a little too old for boyfriend-girlfriend titles don't you think?"

As if everything I've done with Ella hasn't felt romantic to the core. Even when I'm punishing her.

"Sure," Damon says with obvious doubt. "No romantic relationship. Got it."

I don't want this conversation with Damon. She isn't ready. There's no reason this should even be a conversation.

If I start talking about how I really feel, about how serious this could get, then it'll be real, and then there will be no turning back.

CHAPTER 19

ELLA

Kelly's thin, arched brow hasn't budged an inch and it doesn't escape me that her gaze is firmly fixed on Zander's ass.

I scold, comically, "You're shameless."

Her murmur is just as humorous. "And you're fucking that hottie?"

My lips pull up as Trish laughs into her glass and the waiter comes by to drop off our appetizers. Ruze has an impeccable variety, from spring rolls and buffalo cauliflower, to steak tartare and caviar.

I've always loved this place. It's laid back, with garage doors that stay open and let the breeze in. If I had to describe the style I'd say it's botanical boho somehow mixed with a brewery. It's high end and expensive as fuck to attract and keep the clientele … well, the rich and famous.

"The rumor mills were true then?"

"Kind of sort of, maybe." I shrug and pop a bite-size crostini with crab into my mouth so I can't say any more. We talked about heading to his place later this week. It'll be the first time I'll see it. He's unpacked and settled in now and if I'm honest, that makes me nervous.

I'm not sure I want to leave. I'm not sure I want to give up my lifestyle because it's something he isn't sure he wants.

"So … what's the deal for real? We know he was fired."

"How the hell do you know that?" I question and my tone is harsher than I anticipated. Trish's widened eyes are evidence that she's taken aback. "Sorry," I whisper and lean forward, snatching another bite from the plates.

"Is it serious?" Kelly asks, choosing a few pieces of deliciousness and sorting them on her small plate.

"How can it be if he doesn't even have a job?" Trish says, piling on.

I don't consider Trish's sentiment emotionally, only logically when I answer, "He has income and it's not like I'm after anyone for their money."

Trish doesn't bother hiding that she's staring, lifting the martini glass to her lips.

"Well, honey," Kelly says and tilts her head, reaching for a spring roll, taking her time to dip it in the accompanying sauce, not looking me in the eye, "it's not *his* money that we'd be worried about."

There's a bit of a chill in the air all of a sudden. "How did you know he was fired?"

"You know how people talk."

"Well, what else are people saying?"

Trish answers first. "That he's broke but into you."

Broke. In social circles, the word *broke* is blood in the water. "How broke?"

"Just not ... not someone who could afford your lifestyle." Chewing the inside of my cheek, I let her comment sink in. I've never really cared to talk about money. There's a knot of guilt that twists in my stomach when I consider the hand I was dealt. I was born into wealth and then everything was left to me when my father was buried and I was only sixteen years old. The cherry on top is that Kam took over everything, keeping me safe, wealthy, and guiding me through a chaotic world of parasites who were after any cent they could suck from me.

I settle on a simple truth. "I hadn't thought much of it."

"I mean it's not like you need Mr. Moneybags, but it's just something to consider." Her tone reflects the high society's guide to staying elite. In other words, don't marry someone who could be after your money.

"I don't plan on ever getting married again." I decide on another comment to keep my friends, as well as the rumor mills, away from the subject of Zander's bank account. "We're fucking and enjoying each other's company. But this bill," I say and gesture to the meal. "He's paying for it and for all the nights we've been out."

As Trish's expression turns concerned, Kelly states she's getting this tab since Trish got the last.

"How?" she asks bluntly and is rewarded with a jab in her ribs from Kelly's elbow.

"Ouch!"

"The fuck is wrong with you," Kelly hisses in a murmur.

I can only laugh, although that sick feeling remains. Before I can answer Trish, she changes the subject.

"There are other rumors too. Like Kam isn't really your conservator and it's a cover-up. You went to rehab."

I don't say a word, but my eyes are locked on Trish's. "Don't worry, my love, there are so many rumors no one knows what's really going on ... but the biggest rumor is that you tried drinking and fucking your way through mourning, and it ended up with a rehab hangover."

"Your social being quiet since you came back is throwing people off, though." Kelly's comment once again holds a tone. She's good at saying things without actually saying them. The hidden message: I better start posting and filling people in so they stop talking.

"You haven't seen anything, have you?" Kelly asks and Trish answers, "We know Kam isn't showing you the articles. But trust us, it's a good angle."

"What are most people saying?"

"You took a trip down to a private resort. A few do think you went to drug rehab. No one really believes the conservatorship is real. There's a seal on it and since Kam knows the judge and Kam's been telling everyone to mind their damn business and let you enjoy some sunshine ... really people are just wondering if you're mad at them. You've never been quiet before and most people miss you."

"It's just us who know, right?" Trish questions although I'm sure Kam has filled her in.

I nod.

"And what about that hunk over there?" Kelly asks.

Peeking over my shoulder, I catch sight of Zander just as he was glancing at me. Butterflies stir and when he winks at me, I blush violently. It's a sin what this man does to me.

With a simper I tell them, "He's my secret. Anything else out there is PR."

Kelly questions, "So the bit about him getting fired because you were fucking?"

I laugh into my drink, some cucumber mocktail the waitress whipped up. "Well, sometimes PR does reflect the truth."

"Mostly people are just happy to see you back and happy that you might be seeing someone else. Like, that's the chatter. You're back from wherever, you're sober." She looks at her mocktail and playfully clinks it with mine. "And that you're fucking around again and causing all sorts of problems with your security team that you hired to keep people the hell out of your life."

Trish nods with a half smile. "It's a good spin on it, I think." Then she asks me, "If we take a pic, can I post it?"

"Selfies with our mocktails?" I lift my drink in pose.

"Girl gang, bang bang?" Kelly offers the caption.

"Fuck yes."

"Will Kam be all right with that?" Kelly asks and I shrug, quickly popping a cherry into my mouth before saying, "Yeah. I'm sure it'll be fine."

"And what about Playboy?" Trish's question brings my gaze to hers. "Can I get him in the background?"

Another one of him in the background?"

"You know what they say ..." Kelly says in a singsong voice.

Spotted once could mean anything or nothing. Spotted twice together means everything.

"Yeah," I say, pushing the word out with more excitement than I anticipated I'd have.

I wonder when he'll see. Who's going to tell him. I want to know what he'll think of it the most. Maybe I should be more careful, but it excites me that they'll know he's something to me.

"Don't tell him you asked me," I whisper to them.

"Feeling cheeky?" Trish murmurs as she applies a fresh pat of powder to her face.

Shrugging, I tell her, "He looks good."

"He looks damn good," she agrees and snaps her compact closed.

"Smile," Trish says as she snaps a photo. I pop in another cherry garnish just as Trish says, "Wait, one more." Back in position, with a cherry at my lips I pose humorously and then pull it out to smile.

"Hell yes," Trish says and grins. "Check them out."

"Oh, post both those," Kelly suggests.

For a moment, there's nothing but an easy happiness, like nostalgia and old times. A row of hot guys in the background at a bar, one of them I'm enjoying the best sex of my life with. Delicious food at an exclusive local restaurant, with damn good company. Not everyone has as good of girlfriends as I do. With secrets that always stay just that—secret.

"I'm still mad at Kam. Not wanting you to post. I miss your daily rants." Trish's admission is spoken beneath her breath as she types out the caption on her phone. "Done. Posted." She nudges Kelly with her teeth sinking into the bottom of her teeth, placing her phone with the screen facing down on the table.

"I bet every comment is going to be about the cherry and Playboy in the background," Kelly surmises, her gaze pinned to her phone. She barks out a laugh not ten seconds later. "Told you," she states, pushing the phone in my direction.

She is so fucking him.

Omg that cherry *laughing emoji*

Our girl is back

BangBang is right! We see you ladies!

Check out who showed up in the background.

The comments filter in with tags to gossip columns and celebrity outlets, dozens by the minute. There's a flip in my chest and anxiousness I hadn't anticipated.

"Come on," Kelly says, shifting her weight to the other hip. "This has to make you smile."

"It does, it does." I force my tone to be more upbeat. "Just … just wish I could post it too." I don't know why I lie. Maybe it isn't a lie. Ever since the other night, there's been a churning in the pit of my stomach. Like I sent something into motion.

"You're the one who pays Kam. If you want to post, post."

"I agree with Trish. Tell your man over there to get you a phone and just come back. You are back. So … if anyone says shit online, block, block, block, block, block."

"I get why he doesn't want me to … Just the thought of being hammered with questions and seeing that video or pics of us …"

"Kam can filter that out. He has his team."

"I know … I don't know why he is so damn adamant."

"I think it's time you put your foot down." Kelly's seriousness takes me aback. "Or I can put my foot down for you."

Trish has far more compassion, but she doesn't hide the fact that she has her qualms when it comes to my PR. "Everyone failed you; you paid them, and they failed."

"I'm still here, aren't I?" My comment sobers the mood too much, too quickly. "I do want to keep up with everyone again. It's just, I feel like I should be careful ... maybe. I don't know. It's ... it all feels different."

"Look, I didn't want to say anything but the way they handled James's passing was shit. That fixer bitch was dumped from Conntelex."

The temperature of my blood plummets at the mention of that company. They're the most sought-after company for "fixing" situations, images, for planting rumors even. I know Kam still has them on retainer.

"Cynthia, right? Like literally the day you woke up from ... your fall," Trish says, lowering her voice. I didn't fall, I jumped, but I keep that correction to myself. They know what happened. She just doesn't want to say it. "That next morning, she was fired."

"It wasn't her fault that I—"

Kelly's small hand lands on mine. "She handled it poorly. Every step of the way. She was supposed to fix it, and her choice was to ignore it in the hopes it would blow over."

Trish huffs, shaking her head as she taps her phone against the table.

I fumble with how to express anything at all from what happened that night. "I wasn't in the best mindset—"

"You shouldn't have been. You paid people to protect you. And they failed you."

Kelly adds in a whisper, "Even Kam." When my eyes reach Kelly, riddled with shock that she'd talk about Trish's brother like that, she's quick to add, "It wasn't his job and I don't blame him. He was relying on the fixer. What the hell was her name?"

"Cynthia. I'm sure it was Cynthia," Trish states slowly, and then adds, "Even Kam will tell you he made a mistake and he wishes he could take it back."

"Given how easily you two are talking about this—"

"Yeah. We've talked about it behind your back, but only because we love you and we're mad on your behalf. It's not in the tabloids; cross my heart."

"Kam did his job there," Kelly chimes in.

"You should have your fucking phone is all we're saying." Trish's statement is final. "And I've told Kam exactly how I feel about it."

"It wasn't just your phone. It was access to support you had all of your life. They snatched it away. What the fuck did they think would happen?" Kelly's eyes brim with unshed tears and it doesn't go unnoticed that everyone is speaking in whispers now.

"We need chocolate."

"Could we?" Trish says while waving down the waitress, motioning to our drinks.

They're quiet, and in that moment, I remember that night, like it happened just yesterday.

"If she can't stop going off, what else is there to do?"

She wants me to keep asking them for space. Just ask for space, as if they would listen.

Kam's spoken up for me, but he's nervous. He hasn't been this nervous since... well since everything with my father. "You don't know her. She doesn't want space."

It's like I'm a child again, scolded, scared, and watching them fight through a cracked door. I can't even bring myself to move to the bed. Instead I stay on the floor, staring at my hands that won't stop shaking.

"You're supposed to fix this!"

"She can't do what she's told," Cynthia says and she doesn't bother to hide her irritation. "She's not supposed to comment."

"They shouldn't be there for her to comment on."

"Kam, I just need it back." My fingers are still shaking. I call out from my bedroom, not leaving where I am. "Kelly just messaged and she said—"

"Okay baby, but not right now." He brushes me off ... like a child. Like I'm something that can be handled.

I stress, "Kam, I want to look at his picture again and—"

He cuts me off, not even listening. "I just need a moment."

We practically speak over one another as I plead for it

back. "I won't comment. I swear. It's just they tagged me. They keep posting it and tagging me and I—"

"We're going to fix it." He tries to shush me.

"Kam! It's my fucking phone." My voice is raw and it hurts. It hurts from crying, from screaming.

"I'm trying to protect you, Ella," he says, emphasizing each word, his face pained.

Gripping onto his hands, where he's holding my phone hostage, I try to pry his fingers away. "Give it to me."

"No!" Kam's wide eyes look down at me as I fall to the floor, both palms hitting the wood with a loud thud. "Kamden," I cry out, feeling so fucking alone.

"Jesus Christ," Cynthia chides in the background. "Give her another Xanax and take her fucking phone away."

I feel so fucking alone. I don't know what's wrong with me.

I don't hear what Kam tells Cynthia, but whatever it is has her offering a snide rebuttal as the door closes, leaving me sobbing against the drywall.

James. James wouldn't be okay with this.

I've never felt so alone.

CHAPTER 20

ZANDER

My house is a comfortable two-story standalone with a brick front in a neighborhood where the houses are separated with space and tress. It's not that expensive, but it's private.

I chose it for the privacy. It's close enough that we could enjoy each other's company at either house, while having our own spaces.

Damon suggested space, given how quickly things have developed and how their sessions have been carrying on. Space is good. There are times when I won't be there for her and she should know to behave in my absence. She should be strong in solitude, if for no other reason than it would please me for her to do so.

So tonight, she'll sleep without me. Silas has already been

informed to be more vigilant than normal. I keep reminding myself that this is best. That she will benefit from this.

And if not, she has my number and she will tell me. That is the only item on her list while I'm good. To keep her phone on her and use it if necessary.

The sound of heavy footsteps on the back deck, draws my attention.

Damon comes in through my back door, rubbing his hands together. "Damn. Cold out there tonight. And you have me out in it for a card game." He takes a moment to look around before saying, "Nice place."

"It's not even snowing." I pull open the fridge and hand him a beer as soon as he's got his coat off. "How's Ella?"

"Already miss her?" he teases with a grin.

"Fuck off. How is she?"

"You can't always be there for everything, Zander. She needs to be okay without you, you know?"

"I assume that means she's doing just fine."

"Last I checked, she told me she was zoning out with a box of chocolates and some new show Kelly told her she needed to binge."

I nod first and then thank him. "I appreciate it," I tell him before patting the threshold and showing him around the new place.

"It's minimal," he comments.

"I like a modern style with clean lines." Glancing around,

I can count on both hands the number of purchases I made for the dining room and living room combined. There's functionality in the gray suede modular sofa. The set of modern chairs with leather backing and black coffee table were on display in the furniture store, as was the abstract black and white with dark blue faded six-by-six canvas. The dining room is even more bare, with simple clear chairs and a dark walnut table that boasts a knot of a single chunk of wood on the surface.

"Downstairs is where it's at," I tell him, avoiding the hallway and in it, my master bedroom, along with the playroom for Ella.

The dungeon is tucked away in the back half of the basement, and I second-guess whether or not I closed the doors as Damon follows behind me on the newly finished stairs.

"This place is nice. You're renting?" he questions.

"Maybe buying," I half answer, more focused on the closed door than his question.

The first thing Damon says is, "Nice," running his hand down the newly felted poker table. "Dartboard in the back."

"No bar yet, but I'm planning one," I tell him. It's a typical game room although all I have in here at the moment is the table and the hung dartboard. "There's still a number of things I'm looking to add." My gaze wanders to the dungeon but I'm quick to correct it.

Before Damon can say any more, his phone goes off. As

he checks his phone, I check mine and a text comes in.

Ella: Do you have Silas spying on me?

I text her back, *I'm always spying on you my little rulebreaker.*

Ella: I miss you.

Damon comments that Silas just updated him. Ella's doing well. He must have just checked on her, prompting her to message me.

Ella: It's quiet in this house without you.

Zander: If you feel empty, I have ways to fix that

Ella: You're so dirty!!

Her mock scolding makes me grin.

Zander: Be good, I'll be watching you.

I put my phone in my pocket while Damon fills me in on his drive. We set up the card table with two decks. I've been back here more often over the past months ordering furniture, making necessary arrangements and debating on whether Ella would be comfortable here or not. It's starting to feel like home again, like my old place I rented, though I'm beginning to think it will never feel completely right without Ella.

With my mind occupied, Damon moves on to other topics. We're setting out a heaping bowl of chips when Damon asks beneath his breath, "You find anything else?"

"Anything about what?' I ask him.

"About Ella's father."

"Yeah." I've been doing more research on Ella's family

history, focused on the media surrounding the trial. "There's a theory that it wasn't her mother who killed her father's first wife. It was the father."

Damon nods. "Sounds plausible."

"There are a number of conspiracy theories out there. Ella was so young, I can't imagine she would know anything."

"I think it would be best to let that part of her history go, unless she's the one who wants to know more?" he questions.

"I haven't told her. It was just ... something just doesn't feel right."

"Are you done looking now?"

"Not until I figure it all out," I tell him. Maybe I shouldn't dig, but there's a prick at the back of my neck when I think about how she reacted to talking about her mother and father. There's something there, I know there is.

Damon's tone breaks me from the thought. "No murder theory talk while the guys are over for cards."

It's like he's summoned them, because there's a loud knock on the front door. Hustling up the stairs, I get to the door just as there's another knock.

Opening the door wide, I tell them to come on in as Damon's coming up the stairway.

"Damn, nice place," Thomas comments before he's even fully in. Glancing around the place, I think it's nice in some ways, yet cold in others.

"I've got boxes to unpack still, but the game is set up

downstairs and there's plenty of beer.

Alex, Thomas, and Ethan file in one by one, shouting and greeting us with slaps on the back. I've known these guys since high school. Damon had a front-row seat to when I lost my shit over Quincy, but they were there too, in a way. Not so much in my apartment, or guiding me through healthy ways to deal with loss. Just in the way they always have been. They checked in on me, invited me out even when I kept declining. They were simply there and that made all the difference.

We've always been there for each other.

"My girl practically kicked me out," says Thomas when all of us are in the kitchen, choosing our first-round picks for beer. "Begged me to spend a night with you assholes."

Thomas and his girlfriend have been together at least six months now.

"When you popping the question?" Ethan jokes, "She sounds like a smart one."

Thomas just smiles wider, not reacting to the taunt. The way he talks about her, always bringing her up, always smiling when we ask about her ... it's telling. He really cares about her.

"Mine was excited too," says Alex. "She said she wanted to binge-watch this romance show on Netflix. I said I'd watch it with her, but she said she wanted to experience it the way it was meant to be experienced, whatever that means."

"Means it's going to be hot," says Ethan. "So hot she won't want you there to see it."

Alex frowns. "Why wouldn't she want me to see it?"

Ethan comments dryly as we make our way down the stairs to the table. "'Cause if it's one of those historical shows, then you'll have to witness how horny she is for a guy in a tricorn hat." The laughter ricochets in the stairwell and the guys keep it moving, finding their place at the table and twisting off the caps to the beers.

"It's about time we had a poker night," says Damon. "How long has it been since the last one?" Damon was the last one to join this group. When he took me in, I took him in. Now he's one of the crew.

"Too long," I say. Months, at least. I used to love cards. We used to play once a week, and I looked forward to it even when I was with Quincy. It's one of those things you walk away from feeling good. Like the world is right.

At that thought, I check my phone, searching for a message from Ella but find nothing.

As the guys chat and catch up, I open up the security app to find the living room empty. There's a nagging twist in my chest, and I'm quick to search before finding her in her bedroom.

It's too early for her to be in bed.

There's the crack of the deck being shuffled as I tell them I'm headed up to get another beer. The guys are passing around pretzels and making a fucking mess of my table, and only Ethan is in need of another beer.

"I'll get you one."

Taking the steps two at a time, I text Ella.

Zander: Spread your legs for me.

Watching on my phone, I see her get the message and then peer up at the camera before doing as she's told. Each heel digging into the mattress and her legs bent and spread wide as she lays back on the bed.

Just as she's texting me, I test her.

Ella: Like this?

Zander: Fucking beautiful.

The fridge opens, delivering a cool sensation and the two bottles clink in my left hand as I text with my right.

Zander: Pet your pussy for me, I want to watch you come undone for me.

The quality of the camera and the app make it impossible for me to see with enough detail to fully enjoy this. Which is for the best, considering my current company.

I don't have to have an up-close view to know my little bird is being greedy.

Zander: Not just your clit ... I want to see you squirm.

I'm slower in my descent downstairs, satisfied that at the very least, my little bird is focused on pleasure now. She's thinking about coming and obeying, about pleasing me and what rewards I'll give her for being a good girl.

Zander: Good girl.

The sound is off, but as I retake my seat, her back arches

on the bed.

Zander: Come for me, but be still.

My text goes unread for a second and then another.

Just as I'm ready to admonish her, she sees and stills, getting back into position after stripping off her nightgown.

Glancing around the table, all the men are looking at me.

"What'd I miss?"

Thomas fills me in. "I asked about your new place and if you got rid of the one down Route 40?"

"Yeah, it was a rental." I peek down at my phone and smirk at Ella, still playing with herself.

Zander: Dip your finger in. Just one.

"We gonna get back into it?" Ethan questions. "I know you've been busy with work and all. Is this more permanent?"

"I'm not sure yet." With my phone in my lap so I can see, I decide to give her a few minutes to enjoy herself.

I've been vague with the guys about the details with Ella, and The Firm. Too much is still up in the air to get into a real discussion about it, and I don't want to spend a poker night talking about it.

"Once a week sounds good to me. Or every other week." I take a good look at Thomas. "You think every other week would be better with your ball and chain?"

I barely hear his answer as I text Ella to come like a good girl and then clean herself up.

"I like every week. The drive wasn't too bad either."

"Lindsey would binge-watch her show once a week," Alex says. "Especially if you're telling me that tricorn hats are hot now. I don't know if I get the appeal of those kinds of hats."

I offer a short chuckle, focused on my little bird's lips making a perfect O as she finds her release on the bed. Fuck, that's hot. I run my hand down my face. I'm hard as fuck.

"You're going to have to if you want to keep up with her," Tom jokes, and it's another round of easy laughter.

"You all right?" Ethan asks.

"Just work," I answer and when I look up, Damon's brow is arched, his phone tapping on the felt surface.

"Yeah, sometimes," he says. "It would be nice to get a heads-up." His tone is dry and I force the humor to stay in my chest at the realization that Damon just got a scene he probably wasn't prepared for. Or Silas did and informed Damon.

Either way, it's one more reason that they need to leave her to me.

"Just don't go being quiet and ignoring us," Ethan says.

Thomas agrees and I have to reassure them that it's not going to happen. My phone vibrates in my lap.

Ella: Did I please you?

Zander: Always, my little bird. I'm looking forward to fucking your pretty little pussy tomorrow.

Ella: That makes two of us.

Zander: If ever I'm not with you and you want to enjoy yourself, I give you full permission to do so, understood?

Ella: Understood. Thank you, Z.

Zander: Are you going to sleep?

Ella: Yes. I'm so tired.

Zander: Sleep well and dream of me.

Ella: You too, Z. xoxo

"I mean it. You're being weird again. Moving and not telling us until after."

"It's a girl, isn't it?"

"Tell me it's a girl, fucking please. God, just tell me you're getting laid again," Thomas groans and the guys laugh at my expense.

"I'm not ignoring you guys. Just …" I contemplate my next words. "Just a bit busy with a client and I had to make some last-minute arrangements."

"Is 'client' a code word here for something else?" Ethan questions.

Running my thumb down my jaw, I decide to admit it. "Possibly, yeah."

"Damn."

"Holy shit."

"She has you moving and everything?"

The guys make their comments and I let them, not giving them much information at all. Damon's the only one who's aware of my preferences.

It feels damn good for them to know about her, though.

"I'm just glad it's a chick and you aren't avoiding us again."

"Not avoiding you, and let's aim for every other week?" I offer and after a few comments while Thomas shuffles, we all agree to keep game night going.

I pulled away from everyone the hardest after Quincy died, and that's why the card games were so erratic for a while there. It felt fucked up to think about sitting around the table pretending like I was all right when she was gone. It still feels a bit wrong, if I'm honest. The fact that I get to enjoy this, and she doesn't, it'll always carry a certain weight. But if I've learned anything, it's that withdrawing from your whole damn life is as good as being dead yourself.

That's no way to live. Not for me, and especially not for Ella. She has to have her life back, and not just with me. All of it. Friends at her house. Dinners out as often as I can take her. A life.

It doesn't take long, maybe an hour or so before my stomach growls and I realize I forgot about dinner. "Anybody else want pizza?"

"You didn't order the pizza yet?" Damon shoots me a look. "Order it. Now." He points me out of the room with a stab of his finger, and Alex laughs.

"Somebody got hungry," I say, and throw down my cards.

I go back into the kitchen to order the pizza and end up wandering down the hall while I'm on hold. All the way to Ella's playroom.

There are windows high up on one wall, thin ones to let

in a bit of light, but otherwise it's equipped with necessary and custom furniture for play, along with a large antique dresser that I use to store toys in.

I have ... a collection. Some of the more severe instruments will stay in the dungeon in the basement. Two locations for two different purposes. I'm hard again imagining Ella spread across the burgundy padded spanking bench.

I chose that design just for her. It looks expensive as hell and having her perched there, with her ass reddened as she pants, is going to be picture fucking perfect.

The St. Andrew's Cross is in the dungeon, although I debated having it in this room. I think it'll serve us better for punishment.

I took my time, making sure it would be perfect so when she enters this room all she'll have to do is enjoy it.

Still on hold, I meander to the dresser and pull open the top drawer. Counting each accessory in the row of vibrators and dildos. All sizes. All intensities. I could spend an entire day using these on her. In fact, when she comes here, I *will* spend an entire day using them on her. It'll take a few days to truly indulge.

Checking on my phone, she's fast asleep. I hope it'll be a deep, easy sleep for her. offering her nothing but comfort.

The other drawers are filled with riding crops, clamps and restraints. I have a separate rack for the longer implements.

Again it strikes me how torn I am with my little bird.

She's delicate in a way that holds me back. The first day we agreed, I would have shown her this collection. I would have already toyed with her.

There's so much about her, our situation, about us in general that conflicts me.

Even the idea of bringing her here isn't as easy as it would be with anyone else.

It would have to go through Cade. Until the courts dissolve her ruling, everything would require his approval.

If my brother agrees, then there's a process we'll have to follow. The Firm will have to modify my house to fit the judge's orders, which I've taken into consideration, but cameras would be necessary.

However, the toys could fall into a different category regarding her physical health and access to any items that could be harmful. They would need to be involved to make sure no stone is unturned for every item in the establishment she resides in. It's the same thing we did for Ella's property, only I can't do it myself, because it will have to be in compliance to the last letter. There would be no room for error if we made a change of this magnitude.

Shutting the drawer, I'm not clear on how this particular room would fare in that investigation.

We'd also have to request a full psych evaluation for Ella. Cade will need documentation proving that it is her choice, and that she made it of her own free will. He'll also have to attest that he thinks it would be in her best interest, which might be a hard sell.

It's one thing for me to be with her in her home, which has already been vetted and cleared and is a familiar location for providing care. It will be another thing entirely to move The Firm's base of operations here. Even if it is only for a night here and there.

It's a massive inconvenience, in other words.

"Nico's Pizza," a voice says on the other end of the line. "You there? The connection doesn't seem great."

"I'm here." Clearing my throat, I remind myself that my friends are here, that tonight is a night where I don't have to think of all these things. I can't help myself, though. All I can think about, all night, is Ella and how best to handle her. How best to proceed with the concept of "us."

CHAPTER 21

ELLA

"So would you say you're happy with how things have been going?" Kam asks as we stop in front of the large paned windows so I can peek into the boutique shop.

The tissue paper peeking out from the thick, pearly black shopping bag tickles my wrist as I sway to face him.

He nods toward the bag. "Not the shopping. I already know you're happy about the shoes for this weekend's social."

Damon, Kam and, more appropriately, Kelly and Trish said I need to get back on the scene. So long as it goes well, everything else should fall into place. Kam said this weekend is the first piece. If my life is back to what it was, if everyone sees me and there's no sign or evidence that I'm unwell, the judge should be moved to dissolve the initial ruling.

Hopefully. The weekend is step one and I'll be wearing Manolos for the occasion.

"Seriously though, gorgeous." I'm on a mission to pick out a dress that will knock Zander on his ass too. I also bought a small riding crop. It's harmless enough and mostly a gag gift, but I intend to be playful after the party. I'm not exactly sure, but I imagine he'll allow me to amuse myself and then show me what he can do with that riding crop.

My cheeks heat and I nearly trip in my heels. "It been ages," I say, defending myself against Kam's smirk when he catches my arm. "Leave me alone," I answer playfully.

"So ... are you happy?"

"Am I happy? I am."

"With everything ... are you ..." he hesitates but with a deep breath, he presses on as we continue our walk down the storefront. "How are you doing with James's ..." He doesn't say death. He doesn't say it, but I hear it.

To anyone else it may seem like we're a well-dressed couple, out for a luncheon or perhaps they can tell we're only friends. To me, this feels like freedom. Although some thoughts and emotions still feel imprisoned.

"More than I have been. It still ... it still hurts sometimes."

"Are you nervous about anyone bringing it up?"

"Zander will be there," is all I can answer.

"Right." Kam nods. "He'll take care of you, but I want you to know you're handling it well on your own too."

I wish I had a retort that wasn't sarcastic. As it stands, all I'm thinking is that I can now add "grieves well" to my resume.

"If all goes well, we should be able to request a psych eval."

His statement stops me in my tracks, although the bag hanging from the crook of my arm continues to swing.

A thought hits me that I haven't considered. "The Firm would leave?"

"When you pass the eval, two things will happen. The first is that the judge can order their dismissal entirely."

"What about Damon?"

Kam's brow scrunches, not understanding for a moment. And then my concern registers, his eyes widening when it does.

"I want to continue my sessions. I'm not a fool. I'm doing better because of him."

"We can continue their service even if it's not judge ordered.

"The second thing ... we can request a hearing on your conservatorship."

"When would we schedule that?"

"Not until you pass the mental health check and The Firm agrees to their dismissal without complaint."

My heels click on the sidewalk as we near the end of the row, with Tiffany's perched on the corner and the sweet smell of pastries from a Brew & Cap coffee shop we just passed surrounds us.

"One thing at a time."

Nodding, I feel more at ease.

"I'm glad we'll be able to continue with Damon."

"Of course."

"Then he can keep monitoring the weaning."

"Weaning?" This time it's Kam whose pace is troubled.

"From the antidepressants," I clarify.

"I didn't know you were stopping them," Kam states, his voice lowered and obviously bothered by the discovery.

"Damon said some people renew indefinitely as long as there are no side effects since withdrawal can create more ... well, it can make things much worse."

"How are you feeling about that?"

"Good," I respond in the same chipper voice although he arches a brow like he doesn't believe me.

Stopping where we are, with the city at our back and couples surrounding us without seeing us at all, I grab ahold of Kam's hands. "It's all going so well. Just let it happen."

"One last thing." Kam's business tone makes an appearance.

"Uh-oh, my PR is mad with me?"

He huffs a laugh, slipping his hands into his black jean pockets, an attempt to appear casual I would think.

"About Zander," he starts and my pulse drops as a chill I hadn't felt yet creeps through my tweed jacket. I pull it tighter.

"What about him?"

"Everyone loves a love story and you two are cute together."

His comment is unexpected and the smile it brings me is genuine.

"Is he on the same page as you?"

"What do you mean?"

"I saw Kelly and Trish's post, Ella." He tilts his head down, his brow raising, like a father scolding his daughter and I laugh.

"Does he know that you're hinting you're together? Does he want that too? This life and ... the things that come with it."

Memories are a fickle thing. They creep back to me. I remember James confiding in me one night and then I told him everything. For us, it brought us closer. But he knows how it is.

"If you want to come out at this party, you can. If you don't," he says then sucks in a breath and looks off into the distance to the mountains, past the shining windowpanes of boutiques and designer shops. "Just make sure, whatever you decide, that you're on the same page."

"What if I want him to stay a secret? Or he wants that?" My heart does a painful flip. Just the thought of having this conversation with him makes me feel sick. I don't know what Z will say.

"That would be a first."

"We could say he is, without it being real," I offer, taking another peek inside the coffee shop and tilting my head toward it.

Kam nods, leading the way, although what I've just said

seems to concern him.

"He's not really my boyfriend. You know?"

"I know. But no one knows that other than you and Zander, plus The Firm, who are bound by a contract. Because of their ... purpose."

His purpose has passed. He stayed because he wanted to. He stayed for me. The need to defend him rises inside of me, but I don't. Instead I swallow it down and settle on something more simple.

"It's just ... for me ... it's more."

"And for him?" he questions.

"He's been blunt. He's my Dom." I'm surprised how much it pains me to say it. At the same time, I don't think Zander is honest with himself. I think he's holding back. No. I know he is.

"Have you asked him about being more?" I keep my lips firmly in place as I stand at the end of a three-person line, pretending to read off the list of cappuccinos like that's more important. The truth is, I think if I push Zander for more, I could push him away and I don't think I'll be okay if that happens.

Kam presses me, saying, "Maybe you should ask him. You know others will be curious, they'll pry. It's important you're both on the same page."

CHAPTER 22

ZANDER

The keys jingle in my hand, the car alarm confirming I've locked it as I make my way to the back door by the kitchen.

The pressed jacket feels stiff, but it's tailored and, more importantly, Ella chose it. I allowed her to pick my outfit for this occasion. It's a sharp look and well dressed. With black slacks, a dark brown belt, black collared shirt and the gray-blue jacket I'm wearing in this single look, the cost is equivalent to an entire paycheck.

But I promised her, I would stay on her arm, I would escort her and I would wear whatever she wanted.

It's well past sunset and I'm eager to see what she's chosen for herself. Checking my watch, I know we have some time in case she's still running behind like she texted she was.

The lights are on in her kitchen and I let out a sigh of relief that surprises me. I understand what Damon meant about Ella needing time to be alone, but it's damn good to get back to her, to be present and know I'll be kissing her, touching her in ways that'll make her shiver. It's addictive and simply walking in the back door is like getting a hit of my favorite drug.

Every single time. I don't think I'll ever get tired of this.

The moment I close the back door, Kam enters the kitchen, none too quietly. It's intentional, almost as if he was waiting for me.

"Kamden," I say, greeting him with an easy tone that's just as intentional. He opens his mouth, looking like he wants to question me, but I have one first.

"I've been meaning to ask you—when Ella was younger—you two were close?" Standing at the threshold between the small nook and kitchen, he stills, his eyes narrowing. Taking a few steps in, I meet him halfway. "I know she was good friends with your sister. Is that why you took custody?"

He blinks. "I took custody because she needed someone and our families have been friends forever. It was a great tragedy." His mask slips on easily. Public relations 101. "I wasn't about to let just anyone step in. You never know what will happen when someone gets control over a young woman like Ella was ... and her assets."

"Control?" My hackles go up, but I remain poised as he

assesses me. Taking a few steps, I stop behind a chair at the table and grip the back of it.

"I mean regarding her assets. Custody is a tricky issue," he tells me, pulling out a seat, but not yet taking it. His gaze reaches mine as he adds, "When you have as much money as Ella does, it's shark-infested waters."

"That's understandable." I've been waiting to ask him this, and it spills out of me before I can stop it. "Do you know if there's any truth to the rumors that there was foul play with her mother's death?"

Kamden shakes his head like this is the most bizarre conversation he's ever been part of, which can't be true. "Not at all."

"There's a number of theories—"

"Why would you look into that?" His voice is slightly raised and he seems to shake it off, laughing slightly although he doesn't look me in the eye. "That doesn't have anything to do with—"

"There were theories. Rumors that caught my attention after what she said the other day."

That statement makes Kamden pause. He swallows thickly before looking back at me, his mask back on and firmly in place. He knows something. He damn well knows he does.

Ella's kitchen is warm, and Kamden lets out a breath. He leans against the counter and looks at me. "People love a scandal. You know what I think?"

"I don't. I would appreciate it if you told me."

He chews the inside of his cheek. "I think it wasn't her mother who killed her father's first wife. I think *he* did it. I think she took the fall, and he had her murdered in prison." Kam's eyes narrow and his voice lowers. "I also think ... that I'm glad he's dead."

"Zander." Damon enters the kitchen, mid conversation. "Am I interrupting?"

"No," I say and then swallow, not wanting to involve Damon in this. "We should talk later, though," I tell Kam, my grip white knuckled on the back of the chair. There's a cold sweat on the back of my neck.

Whatever happened, I'm almost certain Kam knows every detail. And a part of me wonders, what does Ella know?

The other night, she was anything but okay remembering her mother. If someone hurt her or coerced her ... I don't know what I'll do, but it takes everything in me, in this moment, to calm the rage that simmers inside.

"I wouldn't look too much into it." Kam attempts to reassure me as Damon rounds the corner of the kitchen, opening the fridge and disappearing behind the door.

"Just seemed like there might be something I should know," I say, keeping Kam's gaze as he slips on his jacket.

"We're on the same side when it comes to this. And the part that matters, is that it's over. It's long dead and it should stay that way."

There's a moment between us, but the moment Damon closes the door to the fridge, bottle of water in hand, it's gone.

Kamden addresses Damon first, and then me. "I'm on my way out. Have a good time at the party tonight."

He leaves, and I watch him go.

"You all right, man?" Damon questions. Relaxing my posture and letting out a deep breath, I decide to keep what just happened between Kamden and me. That conversation isn't over.

"Yeah, I'm fine."

"Don't worry about the party. It'll be packed and might be intense for the both of you. But you can always leave." I stare at Damon, unblinking.

"You're my therapist now?" I ask deadpan and instantly the tension in my shoulders lifts.

He laughs, setting the bottle down. "I'm just picking up on the tension is all. You look sharp, she's excited and I think she's ready."

I can't help but to smile at the idea of my little bird being excited. Everything about her is fuller, lighter, happier than she was when I first saw her in the courtroom. Nearly everything. The vulnerability is still there and she's still so very breakable.

Damon adds, "There's no reason to be concerned."

"I'll have a better time when it's over and everything goes well."

The thought of the party doesn't thrill me. There's a delicate balance between us right now and I'm certain she has the upper hand with what to expect with this party. This is necessary, though.

"She told me tonight could set a precedent for the order to be dissolved?"

"That's the plan that Cade and Kamden have agreed on."

"What exactly are they looking for?"

"Returning to normal documented behavior and presenting it to the judge."

"Good." I nod along with the plan. It's ideal. It should be straightforward. And it aligns with what Ella told me, so they're being transparent with her.

"How's she been today?"

"She's been ... seeking pleasure." Damon doesn't look at me, and there's a tilt of his head.

I don't understand at first. "In her journaling?"

"No. Not in her journaling." Damon looks me straight in the eye.

Oh, fuck. *That* kind of pleasure. The kind of pleasure I ordered her to have. Just the thought of her enjoying herself makes my cock stir. *That's my good girl.* "Thoughts on that?"

"It's a good sign that she's doing better."

"That makes me happy to hear."

Damon nods in agreement. "You seem lighter," I comment.

"I think tonight is going to go well. We talked about it

earlier. Ella is ready and looking forward to it."

Before I can say a word, he adds, "She asked me about drinking tonight."

"Drinking?"

"It's a social event. She said she'll most certainly be around it and be tempted."

"What did you tell her?"

"She's weaning off the antidepressants. She should use her best judgment, but a glass would be all right. Maybe sticking to only one drink would be best."

"Sounds good." It does not sound good. I want to close the kitchen door behind Damon, take her upstairs, and strip her clothes off. I want nothing between us but air. And then I want to figure this out. It would be easier if I could breathe her in. Taste her.

Protect her from any pressures that would move her too quickly, too close to dangerous territory.

"You sure you're good with going to the party by yourself?" There's no hint of judgment in Damon's voice. None at all. "I could go, if you want a second pair of hands."

"Silas will be in the parking lot, won't he?"

Damon nods. "He's already there, waiting. I'm off duty and you are officially her chauffeur."

I huff a laugh at my job description and already feel relieved knowing Silas is in place. "I'll be fine. I doubt things will go too late."

"I'll have my phone if you need anything." Damon slaps me on the shoulder on his way past. "Any time, day or night."

"I know it."

"I'm headed out. Seriously—you'll call if you need anything?"

"I'll call."

"Okay. Have a good time."

With the door shutting behind him, there's a feeling that takes over. A need to go to her, to kiss her, to brush her hair to the side and tell her what a good girl she's been. I call her name into the house, and a soft noise from upstairs answers.

She's in the bathroom in her bedroom, the light slanting into the hallway from the open door. I'm drawn to it, and it seems for a second that she's the light source.

The glow inside the bathroom caresses her hair, which has been gently curled and cascades down over her shoulders. Ella leans in close to the mirror, her hips pressed against the countertop, and an animal urge claws at me from the inside out. I could take her like that. I could brace her hips in my hands so they wouldn't get bruised on the counter and command her to watch how beautiful she looks in the mirror while I fuck her.

With my grip on the threshold, I stay where I am, watching her instead.

The light shines off the silver tube of lipstick in her hand. Red, to go with the black dress hugging her hips and skimming her thighs. High heels lift her legs into a criminally beautiful stretch. Is my heart even beating?

Ella finishes and presses her lips together, then blots at the color with a tissue. I have the oddest feeling that I'm watching something out of the past. A memory come to life, right here in this house. This gorgeous woman, in her former glory.

She looks at me over her slender shoulder and shoots me a sultry look as her gaze roams down my body. As if she's the huntress.

How utterly fucking adorable.

"Hey, Z."

"I'd punish you for not greeting me on your knees, but it'd be a shame to wrinkle that dress." Color rushes to her cheeks and there's a glint of mischievousness in her dark eyes. "You look gorgeous, Ella."

"Are you ready?" I ask her.

"I'm as ready as I'll ever be."

It's quiet as I lead her downstairs, her hand tightly holding mine.

The spark between us is magnetized, the air electric as I help her into the car. She's graceful but most of all, quiet.

"Z," her voice murmurs over the hum of the car before we've even left her house. "Whatever happens tonight, just ... you'll still want me, won't you?"

"Why do you say it like that?"

"People will ask questions."

"People are irrelevant when it comes to our relationship."

"You say that," she says and brushes a stray hair from in front of her face. "But what about when they ask if there's anything between us?"

My pulse races with the way she looks at me. As if saying the wrong answer now will stay with her forever. I'm weak in this moment. Weak for her and the thought of her walking away.

"I'll be there when you answer, and whatever you tell them is what I'll say."

"What if I tell them that we're together. That we're … an item?"

"Like I said, whatever you tell them, I'll agree with."

The host, a socialite in the elite circles Kelly entertains, lives at another ritzy house a twenty-minute drive away. Not quite as expansive as Ella's home, but it's up there.

And it's crawling with guests. Expensive cars are parked along the half-circle drive. Music pours out into the front gardens. Chatter is heard from the house and even those gallivanting in the yard. It's a sight to behold. The sheer luxury and expense of the evening doesn't hide behind a curtain. It creates a spotlight for itself.

We haven't been out of the car thirty seconds when my phone buzzes for the first time.

Damon's name is displayed on the screen. I don't have time to check it this second. I need to be aware of what's going on around us and aware of how Ella's behaving. And at this very second, she's ahead of me, in the chaos of the crowd. The sky is pitch black and with everyone around her blurring, she peeks over her shoulder, eyeing me with a happiness I haven't seen from her. One that lights up everything around her.

The phone buzzes again a second later.

Cade.

"Z," she calls out, turning around but not stopping her stride. As she twirls back around, she reaches out for me to take her hand. Hers slips into mine and my phone slips in my back pocket. Let us at least get settled. There's nothing to report just yet.

"How are you?" I check with her as she squeezes my hand.

"Excited," she confesses with a beautiful smile, her teeth sinking into her bottom lip. "You?"

"I'm happy you're happy."

There's a photo op at the front entrance and Ella poses without me, then pulls me in behind her for a shot. A photographer calls out, "Who's the gentleman?" She ignores the question, choosing to wink at him instead.

"Cheeky girl," I tease when she takes my hand again. She's delighted, mischievous and it's a thrilling sight.

As soon as we've relinquished our coats at the door check, a clutch of women I don't recognize descend on Ella, greeting her with shrieks and hugs and so much touching that I angle myself closer to her to give her some breathing room. Her face is lit up with exhilaration, color in her cheeks and a glint in her eyes.

She glances at me. I put my hand on the small of her back and lean down to speak into her ear. "If this is too much, give the signal." Three fingers directly over her lips, the tip of her middle finger resting on the tip of her nose, means I'll immediately intervene.

"I know," she whispers and takes a step ahead of me. I stay back, letting her readjust to something that I'm sure has been familiar all her life. It's almost as if she's the client once again. I'm here to protect her, to shield her. I'm here to offer her comfort if she needs it.

And judging by the sweet laugh that she utters from her lips, she doesn't need me. Not in this moment.

As she looks up at me from under her lashes, my phone buzzes again.

There are more people than I expected. I try to refocus to keep an eye on all of them in relation to Ella.

Another message. I glance down at my phone and see both Cade and Damon are checking in. There's no emergency, nothing to cause alarm.

I text them back, everything going as planned.

A light touch on my arm draws my attention. It's Ella, her dark eyes searching my face. "Can we go somewhere and talk?" Something's off.

"Of course." My answer is irrelevant. Ella's attention is quickly drawn away.

"Ella!"

Trish pushes her way through the crowd to get to Ella's side and wraps her up in a giddy hug. "People are waiting for you. Come on, let's go."

"Who's here?" Ella asks.

"Old friends, new friends ... and everyone worth showing off the new you to."

Trish leads Ella up a flight of stairs and toward the back of the house. I stay a few steps behind but I don't miss how Ella checks on me. Each time she peeks over her shoulder I offer her a calm smile.

"You good?" she mouths at me. As if she's the one who should be worried and not the other way around.

I eye her in a way she should recognize and then tap her ass to keep it moving. Her shy smile and the way she bites her lip are everything. They go out through a set of open double doors. It doesn't make sense that the doors are open—it's too late in the year—until I step out after them.

It's a massive heated porch. On the other side is a long bar.

The partying on this level is far more intense. Trish and Ella join up with a crowd near the bar.

Someone hands her a drink. Someone I don't recognize but Ella obviously does.

"Cheers," the woman yells over the loud din from everyone one else out here, and Ella drinks from her glass. It's only a sip at first, but it doesn't take long for more people and more sips until it's drained along with the rest of them.

"Zander," calls Trish over her shoulder, and I step forward so she can introduce me to their friends. I don't hear any of the names she says while I shake hand after hand, looking into one glazed-over pair of eyes and then another.

They're wasted. Every person here is drinking heavily and as I'm politely shaking hands. Ella accepts another drink. Red flags. This is a sea of red flags.

CHAPTER 23

ELLA

This party feels like a funhouse and I'm in the middle, distorted by all the mirrors, too hot and drunk and a mess.

"Like I said, whatever you tell them, I'll agree with."

It didn't quite hit me at first when he said that in the car, or maybe it did and I just played it off. But the more time passes, the more upset I get. A drink down and he's not beside me. He's staying back and it feels like I'm here alone.

There's a heat, a longing, a stirring of anxiousness that's just getting worse and worse.

I want another drink and then another.

He can't even agree that we're an item? I shouldn't have come in here without dealing with it first, but here we are.

He's stayed back and behind me, not by my side. He's

there, though, I remind myself. He's here, we're just ... I don't know what we are.

With two drinks in, I'm already feeling it, and every passing second he's not by my side, I feel more and more betrayed.

"You good, girl?" Kelly asks, clinging to my side before kissing my cheek.

"Just pissed," I whisper and it takes a second for her to register it, more reading my lips than hearing it over how loud everything else is.

With her brow knitted she asks why, and I nod toward Zander.

All I asked him was what if we were to be called "an item" and he couldn't say that we were. It hurts. I tried to pretend like it didn't, but alcohol has a way of making lies go quiet. I haven't forgotten what Kam said. I haven't forgotten what Damon said.

"Fuck him," Kelly murmurs and then peers across the patio to a hoard of men. Some of them I know, one of them I know-know, and others I don't.

"I don't want them. I want him," I tell her and she nods.

"Maybe a little attention from them and Zander will shape up?" she suggests and I shake my head. "I'm not ... no. I don't know." My head is fuzzy.

Minutes pass and more people gather. Only one person mentions James. With everyone talking over each other, it barely registers. I only know it was spoken to me because the group around me goes quiet. I stare back at a tall man, his hair cropped back and his tie loosened around his neck.

"Just, I'm just ... I wanted to give my condolences is all."

My heart does that pitter-patter thing. Before I can even answer, Zander's on one side of me, telling me someone named Arthur is looking for me and Kelly's on the other side, a flute of champagne that was in her hand, being pushed into mine.

"Drink up, baby."

It feels like stumbling, as I turn my back on the group, Zander's arm around my waist as he leads me away.

"You all right?" he questions and I throw the flute back, letting the bubbles worm their way down my throat.

My eyes prick and suddenly everything isn't so great and wonderful.

"It fucking hurt," I say to him and breathe out, but not daring to look him in the eye. If I do, I think I'll lose it. The one night of all these nights where I need to simply be and be seen, and this has come over me.

"I know," he says and then I realize he's talking about James. Fuck, it's a knife to the chest. I struggle to respond at all. In a sea of people, I glance around them, feeling the cool breeze against my hot face, and I feel alone. With the exception of this man.

"Do you love me?" I ask him, barely breathing.

His striking eyes hold me for a moment, and I think he'll admit it. He has to feel it, doesn't he? He speaks his words carefully. "Ella, you're drunk."

I've felt my heart break before. I've felt it shatter. It belonged to someone else back then. Someone who would never dare to hurt it. "Don't do this. Not here."

"Right," I answer him in a single breath, attempting to compose myself. Swallowing thickly, I push it all down. All I can hear are my heels clicking on the ground as slow as my heart beats.

With my heart beating faster, I walk with him and accept the bottle of water. "No more drinks," he orders. "Only water."

Fiddling with the cap, I nod in agreement.

Why does it hurt as much as it does? It feels like the rain has poured down around me.

All because he couldn't say we're an item?

No. No it's not that. It takes me minutes to register that I asked him if he loves me.

He knows. He must know, that I love him. Fuck, I am drunk. I'm far more than tipsy.

The conversation plays on repeat. Then the one with Kam insinuating we aren't on the same page. Then the one with Damon, and how my feelings may be displaced.

"We're going to steal her, if that's all right." Kelly's voice rings clear over my head in the dark corner behind the bar that Zander's cornered me into.

"I think it may be time for us to head out."

"You just got here." Kelly's objection reflects both her

shock and disappointment.

"I'm not leaving. I'm fine." My voice is clear and my decision firm as I look Zander in the eye.

"So ... about stealing her away? I think she should see some people. Some influential people Kam mentioned?" she tells him. Asking *him* permission and not me.

He doesn't answer her, other than to nod. There's a concerned look in his eyes and he tells me, I'll be right behind you.

"I'm not letting her out of my sight," he warns Kelly who only laughs, a sweet friendly sound before whispering to me that whatever he said he can shove up his ass and that she loves me.

"Should we hide in the bathroom?" she asks me and I shake my head. Half of me wants to leave, while the other half wants to feel it, and let it all go.

"Smile on," she says and like a ghost taking over, I grin entering the room and hollowing out to let the former me show. That's what this night is about. This is for me, not him.

As the clock ticks by, and hour passes easily, I laugh when everyone else does. I smile for the cameras. I accept hug after hug and give comments to the gossip columnists when they ask for one that would make Kam proud. I've been through hell and back. If Zander thinks his commitment problems are enough to break me, he's the one who's got a new thing coming.

I'm fine. I'm better than fucking fine.

He's barely approached me, watching from a few feet away as if he's merely security. He must know he fucked up. He called in backup. I spotted Silas across the room and nearly rolled my eyes. It's yet another betrayal. It fucking hurts. It feels like a breakup. Like I did the one thing I knew I would do. I pushed him and he refused to move with me.

I have issues, yes. But so does he. And it's not my responsibility to take his problems on. That's what I tell myself anyway, as I'm looking at my ex from another life.

That ... and to do what Kelly suggested, to show Zander why he needs to commit.

John, a handsome lover from years ago, circles the edge of the crowd, his face disappearing and reappearing as people talk into my ear and ask me the same stream of questions over and over. *How are you? Are you settled at the lodge? We missed you.*

I just wish it didn't hurt so much to be here hearing how much they missed me and being reminded over and over that I was gone. Being reminded of what happened.

Suddenly, the music feels like an assault, and the crush of their bodies close to mine, and the heat of all that skin so close by. The autumn night can't compete with the number of people here and it's too much. It was easy to be irritated at Zander before, when he kept pointing out that we could leave any time, when he insisted on going over our signals again and again, and now it turns out he's right.

I hate that. It feels like a rock at the pit of my gut to be wrong about this. But if I'm being honest, it's not the party that feels like such a raw, open wound. It's him. I had him in my bed, where I thought he belonged, and he didn't choose me.

Tears prick at the corners of my eyes but I blink them away before they can fall.

"You need another drink." Trish's face swings in close, her eyes bright.

"Hell yes I do." Zander's order be damned.

She throws her arms over her head and cheers, and I echo it. My voice is too weak to do it justice but it doesn't matter. The music is loud enough to cover it up. The music is loud enough to cover everything up, except Zander.

I can feel him watching me. His eyes on my skin are a palpable burn, even when I can't see him through the crowd. I know he can see me.

I don't look at him at all. It's one of the more difficult challenges of my lifetime, keeping my eyes away from his. Screw him. I don't want to look back at him and see all that emotion in his eyes. It's bullshit. It's not for me.

Trish comes back with two shots and we knock them back together. Oh, it's a bad idea. She pulls me into the circle of friends and into an argument about which shots are better, and who would rather have a full mixed drink, and who's really a wine girl.

"Wine," I hear myself say. "I know I just took a shot, so it doesn't make any sense. I love wine at the end of the day."

Trish agrees with me, and it becomes reality—I'm still a woman who loves a glass of wine at the end of the day. It's a lie. It's not true. There's no wine in my house, and even if there was, drinking too much of it makes my throat hurt. I love the idea of having wine at the end of the day but I don't love the reality. Which thing is more real?

I love the idea of being with Zander but not the reality of him rejecting me. Of him choosing to guard his heart over protecting mine, or his past over me, or whatever he's choosing.

Maybe he loved Quincy so much, he'll never love again.

Maybe I should be like that. Maybe James should be my one and only love.

"Another shot!" Kelly calls out and I don't hesitate to down it.

I thought Zander would choose me. I thought he wanted me. I've been over his lap, I've had his hands everywhere on my body, I want it now.

I want it now.

I want all of it. The conversation floats around me and none of it sinks in. I'm pushing past comfort for my voice, so

I stop answering questions and put on a big, fake smile.

No one notices.

Not a single person notices that I'm broken, and that I'm desperately sick of being broken. I'm so tired. It's a tiredness that sinks into my bones and weighs me down to the floor. I'm so damn heavy with it.

"Hey, sweetheart."

John. My ex. He's not like Zander, not dark and handsome. He's blond and beautiful and an all-American kind of guy who could be in a men's magazine. I tip my face up to look at his. "Hi."

We broke up a lifetime ago, right after college. Two different people going two different directions, we said. It took me by surprise, though. I'm always the one who's surprised. I never see it coming. But who cares about all that? He's standing in front of me right now, and Zander's not. Zander didn't want to be in that place.

"It's been a while since I've seen you out. How are you?"

"Better now that you're here to talk to." I touch his wrist, a little flirtatious touch, just so Zander will see. "Some of these conversations." I roll my eyes.

"I know." John shakes his head.

This is how we were. Other people had conversations, and we were better. Up until the day John decided he was better than me. Times are different now. I'm the one with all the mystery. I could cry from how ironic it is. The worst things in your life end up making people more curious about you. I had money before, but now I have whispers and rumors and the ability to turn heads just from walking into a room.

"You look like you could use a drink."

"I do need one."

Another lie. Lies on top of lies on top of lies. When is Zander going to step in? When is he finally going to choose me? I know I'm pissing him off every time I put a glass to my lips. I know it, and he's not doing anything at all about it. I edge closer to John and let him take me to the bar for another shot. I let him lift it to my mouth for me and put my arm around his waist when he tips it up so I can drink.

Choose me.

Just choose me.

He doesn't.

John starts talking to me about his job, about all the bullshit conversations that go on there, and I make up a story. I make up a story where I'm not under care in my own home, and I'm not struggling every day to keep my head above water, and I'm not suffering through this party with a broken heart because Zander didn't want to be with me the way I want to be with him.

Zander doesn't enter into it at all. I never mention his name. I don't say that he's the man who's been watching me this entire time. I don't say that it's foolish of me to want him the way that I do, because it's not allowed. Because he's always been forbidden. I don't say any of it.

I bottle it up and touch John's arm and his waist and I throw my head back and laugh at his stupid jokes even though it hurts my throat to do it. I take another shot even though I'm already too drunk, already past the point where I should have stopped and gone home.

A dark-haired woman who looks put together and not very drunk at all steps between John and me, getting his attention. She has perfect red lips and a dress that's cut low in the back. She looks hot, and I'm a mess. I'm a mess who wants Zander and wants her life back and maybe I'll never get it. Maybe I'll only have Zander in my bed and I'll never get to have him and I'll always be this person who wants what she can't have. Who wants it so badly she breaks her heart every day of her life thinking about it.

"Sorry about that," John says. "You all right?" he asks with humor in his tone and a short laugh. He cups my chin, and his touch is warm.

"I'm fine," I whisper and then clear my throat.

"You look sad that I left you."

I lie. "I was."

His shoulders rise with a pride and wanting I've seen from him before. He leans in close to whisper in my ear. "I guess I shouldn't leave you alone again then."

Alone.

Zander's so far away that he left me alone.

My heart tinks.

"I need some fresh air." The air in this covered patio isn't enough for me. It's too warm and too full of other people. On one end of the bar there's space. The gap between the bar and the railing is so narrow here that the bartenders can't fit on this side. Oh—one of those L-shaped bars. I see it now.

"Remember how we used to let it all go?" I ask him, eyeing the edge of the railing.

John grins and asks, "You want to?"

I only nod, feeling my heart race.

It was a different time and for different reasons. But right now, it's all I want to do. Let it all go.

John helps me hoist myself up on the other side, abandoning the shot glass I've been holding, and stand up.

I'm so hot, and I can't be hot anymore.

"You ready?" he asks at the same time that I hear Zander shout out. As I close my eyes, he's there, staring from so far away.

All it takes is two steps.

One step to the edge of the bar. The next step to the railing.

Two steps. One jump, and I'm sailing through the air, off the side of the railing, going down fast.

CHAPTER 24

ZANDER

"E lla!"

She disappears.

Drops out of view.

One second she's there, the next she's gone, and I lose my mind. I don't know who it is that I shove out of the way. One guest, maybe two, and then the bartender.

"The fuck are you?" some prick questions as I fist his shirt and shove him back. He's the one who helped her up, some asshole she decided to punish me with.

No one's screaming around me. The air isn't filled with terror. They're cheering. Pure delight electrifies the air.

My heart is in my throat, caught there along with my voice. I can already see the blood when I reach the bar and hurtle around. My legs slam into the railing on the side of the balcony. My hips connect. I lean out over the drop—I have to see if she's still alive, and ...

It's a pool.

There's a pool down below. Ella floats in the middle of the pool, kicking her feet and pushing her soaked hair back from her face.

My beating terror screams itself into anger.

"It's a fucking pool, man." The asshole who helped her up dares to fucking speak to me.

Gripping his collar with both of my hands, I look the son of a bitch in the eye and warn him, "If you ever touch her again, it'll be the last thing you do."

What the hell was she thinking? My hands shake as I storm my way down, ignoring the gasps and onlookers.

I was already counting the ways I'd redden her ass. I was already cursing myself for taking it too easy on her. For not being more forceful. I'd let her push and throw her tantrum. I'd let her get it out of her system and when we got back home ... I'd show her who she belonged to.

If she wants me to say it, I'll fucking say it. I want her, I need her. I have love for her that I don't anyone else. I can't lose her. Yes. I'll tell her I love her.

My blood rushes in my ears. My hands fisted and every muscle in my body is coiled.

I let her get away with too much all because I was waiting

on Damon or Cade to get their asses here. Why the fuck did I listen to Silas and wait for The Firm?

She's mine. She misbehaved. I'll be damned if I let this situation get in the way again.

Taking the stairs as fast as my feet will carry me, not a single thought in my mind is spared for anyone else at this hellish party. Not one. All I care about is getting to Ella. I need to secure her safety, I need to get her out of here, and I need to punish her for what she's done. I need to make her understand what she's done to me.

It's cold out by the pool, with heat from the water rising into the air.

And I'm not the first one to arrive.

I don't know how the hell that fucker got here, but there he is, helping her climb out of the pool and laughing. Peering up at the house, I see an iron spiral staircase down just on the other side where the bar was.

The two of them laugh like this is funny, like my heart hasn't been ripped out of my chest and beaten. They're a pretty match like that. A young couple, in each other's arms, pretending that life is a joke. One of them hasn't been wounded. One of them doesn't feel like a madman.

None of it matters. I can't stop. I get there just as he's leading her away from the pool and take her by the shoulders.

"Fuck off," I spit out. "I told you to stay the fuck away from her."

"Hey man," he says and reaches for Ella who doesn't spare him a glance.

"I thought you didn't want me," she says. As if I've ever not wanted her.

His eyes go wide, darting between us. "Have you fucked him, El?"

I'm dimly aware of cameras around us. Cameras and phones. Recording. We need to get the hell out of here. "It's not like that," Ella says. Her voice is soft at the margins. She's been drinking.

I lean in, looking him dead in the eye. "She's mine."

"Z," she says and her voice is broken. I know I didn't say the things she wanted. But I'll be damned if I don't fight for her to give me a chance to make it right.

She's fucked up. I'm fucked up, but together we work.

"We're leaving." I see the opening in the crowd and move us toward it with Ella tucked tight into my side, my arm across her shoulders.

Her pace barely keeps up with me. If I didn't think someone would call the cops, I'd throw her ass over my shoulder.

"Zander," she says, her voice barely audible over the noise from all these people talking, talking, talking. They make so much noise. "Zander, stop."

"Not a chance in hell."

It takes forever to get us through the house. The crowd

seems to have multiplied and all of them want to be in our way. In my way. Ella's not helping. Every time she turns her head, she sees someone else she wants to talk to and tell them it's fine. I can't find the words to make her understand the situation we're in. She jumped off a second-floor bar and into a pool below.

She could have died.

She could have *died*.

Cade and Damon both said the same thing. Don't make a scene. They said they'd be there after she took the first shot. A fucking half an hour and a goddamn heart attack later and they still aren't here.

"Zander," she protests as I pull her along, her long legs and heels not keeping up with my strides. I swear I'm two seconds from throwing her over my shoulder. I can barely contain myself.

I can feel myself falling into that old spiral. It's the same thing that happened after Quincy died. I questioned every action I ever took, trying to figure out which one would have kept her alive.

I can't do this again. I cannot fall into that shit again. It almost destroyed me the first time.

"We need our coats," Ella says as we make it to the front entrance. "Coats!" she yells out and everyone around us takes notice. "You're acting like a maniac," she scolds me under her breath.

Soaking fucking wet, dripping from head to toe, somehow still gorgeous, she dares to tell me that I'm the one acting like a maniac?

My exhale is long and audible as I stare down at her. "We need our coats," she repeats clearly and I swear I'll lose my mind if I don't get her out of here and across my lap in the next five seconds.

There are dozens of coats here now. Maybe over a hundred. I park Ella at the door of the coat closet and dig through them.

"We don't have to leave," Ella says from behind me, her arms crossed, onlookers watching her calmly berate me. *I swear to God.*

Cade and Damon's directions about not making a scene are fucking hysterical by now.

My coat appears and I toss it in Ella's direction. It's another fifteen coats before I find hers. Step over to her. Put it around her shoulders. I take my own coat by the collar, and take Ella by the arm.

"Z," she says and the single letter is a plea on her lips.

"I'll deal with you when I get you alone." I'm too loud and too obvious, and from somewhere nearby I hear the click of a shutter. I don't care. Anyone who takes a photo right now is taking a photo of a bodyguard doing his job.

"Zander, please calm down," she insists, her voice getting rougher. It's been too much. This night out has been too much for her. At least the last round of shots were water, courtesy of the hefty tip I paid the bartender, but still. I should have put a stop to it earlier. The second she asked me if I loved her, the words slurred on her lips, we should have been out the door.

The only thing that kept me here was the fact that she needed this. She needed everyone to see her. It was going so perfectly. Fucking hell.

I guide Ella out the front door and down the steps. Maybe it will look like a jealous man taking a woman out of a party before she's ready.

I'm not jealous. I'm beside myself.

Ella doesn't say a word on the way to the car. The cold is setting in. She shivers under my arm, wrapped in her coat. Her teeth click together as we reach the car. I bundle her into the passenger side and run around to mine and throw myself in. Start the car. Turn the heat all the way up.

The tires screech as I back out of the parking spot. I don't bother to call or text a soul seeing as Silas is standing right there at the exit, watching us leave.

The radio plays along as I accelerate into the road and get us out of the neighborhood, thankfully, Ella reaches over and turns it off. I usually took city streets between the motel and Ella's, but tonight I take the first available turn onto the highway that skirts the edge of town. Stars shine above the mountain in clear skies. *What was she thinking, jumping off that bar? What the hell did she intend to do to me?*

Ella huddles in the passenger seat, her teeth clicking together with her shivers. Her arms lock tight around her stomach. "I'm so cold."

I try to turn up the heat some more, but it's already at full blast. "That's probably from jumping off of a balcony into the pool when it's freezing outside."

I don't take my eyes off the road for even a moment and focus on not losing it. It doesn't matter. I can still feel her watching me.

"Are you mad at me?" she whispers as the night whips by us.

Mad does not begin to describe what I feel right now. It's such an intense storm of emotions that I hesitate to open my mouth. There are no words to describe it. Mad doesn't encompass the terror and the relief and yes, the anger.

It doesn't describe the need.

Because right now I am in a state of need. I need her to understand. I need an outlet for all these things I feel. I need to be in control.

I don't answer, and Ella doesn't ask again. She stares through the windshield as we sail through the night, headlights from the oncoming traffic gliding across her face at uneven intervals.

We pass the exit we'd have to take to go to her house.

I feel Ella notice it. Her wet clothes shift against the seat. But she doesn't ask the question. On some level, she already knows where we're going.

The exit that leads to the motel looms out of the night, and I give all my attention to driving carefully. To steering us off the highway and going the speed limit and not fucking up another thing tonight.

We're here. The mom-and-pop motel is a strip of rooms on a quiet road off the highway. It was closer than my house, closer than hers. And we'll have privacy.

Lights burn on the outside of each door, keeping the night at bay. I think it's meant to be welcoming, but right now it's more than welcoming. It looks like safety. There's no one outside the rooms.

I park, and leave her where she is.

"Stay while I get a room," I order and she nods. For a moment, a tic in my jaw spasms until she answers, "Yes."

Once I have the key, I open my trunk to take out a spare bag that stays there. Most of it is useless, but there's a dry undershirt and pair of boxers that will do. Grabbing them, I go around to her door. Wordlessly, I open it and offer her my hand.

Ella hesitates.

Then she puts her hand in mine.

That hesitation does something to me. I know she's delicate. But I also know had I been stricter, this shit wouldn't have happened. She wouldn't be questioning a damn thing between us.

I hustle us to the door, take the key out, and let us in.

The room seems too small to contain me in this moment, but there's more than myself to focus on. "Get out of those wet clothes."

Ella stands by the door, still and silent, and I unbuckle my belt. As I pull it apart, ready to slide it through the belt loops, I see she hasn't moved an inch.

"Little bird."

Her eyes snap to mine.

"Get out of those clothes."

I don't know if it's because she's responding to me or because it's cold that Ella's fingers go to work on the buttons of her coat. She strips it off and tosses it across the table, then goes for the hem of her dress. Anger surges through me again. She could have died, and then I would have been there with her broken body and my broken soul. She could have died and left me to live through the aftermath.

Ella has her dress over her head, her bare breasts perky, her nipples pebbled. She's not entirely steady. Probably still drunk, and how the hell did I let that happen? I told her there would be punishment for drinking. She knew that going in. And she did it on purpose.

Which could mean—

I don't know what anything means anymore.

The rest of her clothes come off, and Ella stands naked by the door of my room. I stalk across the too-small space and grab a clean towel out of the bathroom, then return to her. "Dry yourself off."

She follows orders with a sullen set to her chin. Ella's got a lot of nerve to be pissed at me in this moment. Like it's my fault that she threw herself into a pool on a cold night. Like it's my fault she threw herself at her ex-boyfriend.

Ella hands me the towel with that same tension in her chin.

Handing out the spare shirt and boxers, I tell her, "Put these on."

When she's pulling the clothes on, I sling her coat over the radiator.

I turn back to find her looking at me, her eyes huge and questioning and pissed. "What am I here for, Z?"

"You know why we're here."

"Why don't you just drop me off at home and leave me?"

"Leave you?" The incredulity is palpable.

"You don't want me. I know you don't."

With a deep, steadying breath, I dare her to call me a liar. "I want you more than I want anything, Eleanor."

My words bring her lips to part and a shuddering breath leaves her. I close the space between us, splaying my hand against her back. "The fact that you question that at all tells me I failed you. But my little bird, you are here because it's time for a punishment that I don't want anyone to see. I intend to fuck you into the early morning, and it's only for us. Everyone else needs to get the fuck out of what we are until you know damn well that you're mine."

Her breathing picks up, her chest rising and falling chaotically and her beautiful gaze caught in mine. My heart beats wildly, knowing that look and that need. Knowing this is exactly where we're supposed to be.

"Z," she whispers.

"You need someone to fuck the wild out of you," I growl, and it's wrong. I know it the second I say it. Ella's eyes fly open, her lips part, and the shock on her face tells me I've screwed this up. I've stumbled over a hidden pain I didn't know existed.

As she pushes me away, my phone goes off.

I ignore it. "You okay?" I question her as she crosses her arms and moves toward the bathroom, everything changed. Something's wrong.

She nods, but doesn't speak it.

"Ella," I start and my phone goes off again. Again I ignore it.

"Ella, look at me," I command her and she does as she's told, her wide eyes staring back at me. "Are you all right?" I question, already knowing she's not.

My phone rings in my pocket and I reach for it without thinking. "What?" I snap into the phone.

"We have a problem," Damon says. "There are photos of you and Ella at the party and—"

"I need tonight, Damon," I cut him off.

I turn my body away from her, as if that will give me any

privacy. As if it will stop her from hearing this conversation. "We need a moment. We can talk—"

"Photos of you two. At the party. They're on social media. There's a story already posted. Several outlets are picking it up. She's not nobody, Zander. What happened? You need to tell me what happened so I can figure it out." Damon's worry amplifies a different concern, one I wish had waited.

Wood knocks against wood, and I whirl around to find the space by the door empty, the door banging against the frame.

Fuck! I run out of the room, dropping my phone and race to the end of the hall. I could have gone left or right, I chose left and I chose wrong. With no one there I race to the other side and find that empty too.

"Ella!" I cry out, desperate for her to come back. *Fuck. Fuck.* "Ella!"

ELLA

"I'm going to fuck the wild out of you, El." James's whispered words echo in my mind. Tears stream down my face and I can't stop them. Huddled into a ball in the corner of some utility closet, I don't really know, it's so dark, I'm rocking back and forth. All I can do is cry, grieving for a man who loved me truly and deeply.

My hands tremble, my body's shaking. With my hair stuck to the side of my face, I let the cold seep in. Needing to feel anything at all. I've gone numb. Numb all over.

I feel it happening again, this darkness that takes over as I gasp in air and wish it would all stop. I'm slipping backward faster than I ever could have imagined.

In the distance I hear Zander calling my name. Once, twice, then it fades. At least it gave me a moment to breathe.

I don't want to be this way.

It was a moment. Only a moment.

There's only one truth that I know as I sit here in the cold dark. I'm not okay.

The National Suicide Prevention Lifeline is a United States-based suicide prevention network of over 160 crisis centers that provides 24/7 service via a toll-free hotline at the number 1-800-273-8255. It is available to anyone in suicidal crisis or emotional distress.

About the Authors

Willow Winters

Thank you so much for reading my romances. I'm just a stay at home Mom and an avid reader turned Author and I couldn't be happier.

I hope you love my books as much as I do!

More by Willow Winters
www.willowwinterswrites.com/books

Amelia Wilde

USA today bestselling author of dangerous contemporary romance and loves it a little too much. She lives in Michigan with her husband and daughters. She spends most of her time typing furiously on an iPad and appreciating the natural splendor of her home state from where she likes it best: inside.

More by Amelia Wilde
www.awilderomance.com/